"A gifted writer who can create and sustain tension with spare, unembellished prose." —*New York Times Book Review*

"In what I like to consider a one-man mission of 'literary reparations' . . . Richard Wiley appears not necessarily to integrate but to insert himself unobtrusively, a watchful eye and empathizing listener, into alien identities, operating through plain, credible protagonists." —**Wole Soyinka**, Nobel Laureate in Literature

"Richard Wiley writes like he was born and raised everywhere." —**Charles Johnson**, author of *Middle Passage* and *Taming the Ox*

"If there is such a thing as global fiction, Richard Wiley is writing it." —**Russell Banks**, author of *The Sweet Hereafter* and *A Permanent Member of the Family*

"Richard Wiley has given us a fascinating and utterly convincing portrait of a young man caught between two cultures and struggling to understand both." —**T.C. Boyle**, author of *The Tortilla Curtain* and *The Harder They Come* on *Festival for Three Thousand Maidens*

"Richard Wiley is a first novelist with the potency and daring of a master." —**Michael Herr**, author of *Dispatches* and *Kubrick* on *Soldiers in Hiding*

Richard Wiley

Bellevue Literary Press
New York

First published in the United States in 2016 by
Bellevue Literary Press, New York

For information, contact:
Bellevue Literary Press
NYU School of Medicine
550 First Avenue
OBV A612
New York, NY 10016

© 2016 by Richard Wiley

This is a work of fiction. Characters, organizations, events, and places
(even those that are actual) are either products of the author's imagination
or are used fictitiously.

Library of Congress Cataloging-in-Publication Data
is available from the publisher upon request

Bellevue Literary Press would like to thank all its generous
donors—individuals and foundations—for their support.

 This publication is made possible by the New York
State Council on the Arts with the support of Governor
NYSCA Andrew Cuomo and the New York State Legislature.

National Endowment for the Arts This project is supported in part
by an award from the National
Endowment for the Arts.

Book design and composition by Mulberry Tree Press, Inc.

Manufactured in the United States of America.
First Edition

1 3 5 7 9 8 6 4 2

paperback ISBN: 978-1-942658-16-0

ebook ISBN: 978-1-942658-17-7

For Cairo Morgan Albert

I have a little shadow that goes in and out of me,
And what can be the use of him is more than I can see.

—Robert Louis Stevenson

PART

ONE

Chapter One

1

WHAT BLURRED THINGS from the beginning with Bob was that Dr. Ruby Okada hadn't believed he was an inpatient in her psychiatric clinic, but simply a man come to visit one. On the night she met him, in fact, she was hurrying off for dinner with another psychiatrist, her friend and colleague Bette, in order to discuss what Bette quaintly called "the strange case of Archie B. Billingsly," a man she believed to be weighed down with such a dazzling array of dissociative disorders that she wanted Ruby's help in writing about him.

Ruby had promised to leave the hospital by 8:00 P.M., but it was 8:30 before she got to the elevator, and the restaurant was a ten-minute walk away. A man in a fine tweed jacket pressed the elevator button for her, and when he said "Late night?" though she didn't know it then, it changed the trajectory of her life.

"It is," she said. "And Bon Bonito has never seemed so far away."

That alone was odd for her. She wasn't sociable with strangers.

The man's hair was long and tucked behind protruding ears. He had far-apart eyes, and an accent that she couldn't place.

"There are three bonito fishing seasons in Samoa," he said. "The best corresponding to the breadfruit season."

"Breadfruit?" said Ruby. "When my father first came here from Japan, he tried to grow breadfruit in our yard."

Her father's failure with breadfruit was one of her earliest memories.

"We carry our cultures with us when we travel," said the man, "food most primarily. The Swedes with their lutefisk, we Scots with our haggis."

Ah! she thought. Scotland, of course!

He stayed with her when she got to the ground floor, exited the elevator, and stepped outside onto the street. She considered waiting until he chose a direction before going the other way, but she didn't have time. "I'm late to meet a friend," she said. "I hope you don't mind if I'm not very talkative."

"Carroll's rabbit could run at breakneck speed, all the while chatting his head off," said the man. "And who can forget how Peggotty gossiped while cleaning the house?"

He jogged when she did, crossing streets with her against the traffic.

"You're a scholar, then?" she asked. "Using obscure references, even for the general public?"

"Not in the least a scholar, and you knew my references perfectly well," he said. "I'm sure that you are the intellectual of your family, with laurel wreaths heaped upon your head."

She stopped so she could look at him properly. Who spoke like that? Still, she couldn't help letting him know that she'd read *David Copperfield* in her tree house when she was twelve years old, and had once known *Alice in Wonderland* nearly by heart.

To her surprise, he grew serious. "To know something

nearly by heart has its ups and downs," he said, "for hardship resides in that *nearly* part."

"Who *are* you," she asked, "and why are you walking beside me?"

A smile broke loose from her face. This was really so unlike her! But she was drawn to his oddness, and could not stop staring at those far-apart eyes.

"I might as easily ask why you are walking beside me," he said. "If two are riding side by side, the leader and the side-kick, can the sidekick think that he's the leader? Can he possibly be that thick?"

He smiled back at her, but also at his own cleverness. It had been years since she'd been so attracted to a man. She had the urge to tuck a strand of wayward hair behind his ear. She could see Bon Bonito a half a block away, a torn end of its awning flapping in the wind. He saw it, too, and pointed. *"It's a handy cove, and a pleasant sittyated grog-shop,"* he said in an entirely different voice.

The last thing she remembered saying that evening was "What?"

2

AND NOW SEVEN MONTHS LATER, the comeuppance.

September 2, 2012

Dear Bette,

I've printed out my resignation letter and placed it in Dr. Spaulding's mailbox. I put a copy on your desk, too, and another on Lou's, in the business office. Lou will be disappointed and Spaulding may even try to talk me out of it, but what will you feel, Bette? You, with your ever-present sarcasm and cut-to-the-chase attitude. Will you feel it serves me right for thinking Bob was Bob for the entire three weeks we were together, when you could have told me in a glance that he was Archie? Or will you feel something like sympathy for my humiliation, for my having fallen so deeply in love with a lie and a ghost, thus proving beyond anyone's doubt that my emotional life has always been a shambles and will never be anything else? I absolutely know that you'd applaud me for deciding to take Archie's house when it was offered, that you'd applaud it a lot more than I do myself, for at least half the time I feel like a fraud.

Because it's Labor Day weekend, I didn't have to meet Lou or Spaulding, nor put up with the residents when I delivered the letters and cleaned out my office. A few of them were around, the residents, but they rushed by me like the rabbit in Alice in Wonderland *. . . "busy, busy, busy," or whatever it was it said. Ah, but mentioning that rabbit just brings me back to Bob again. Though I've spent a lot of energy trying to extract him, I've been no more able to do that than take measures to extract the seed he planted inside of me when there still was time. Some women could have done that with ease, but I'm not one of them. Does that make me an antifeminist, on top of everything else?*

At any rate, this much is decided: I will leave my apartment but will stay in Archie's house until my baby's born. Dad will come out for the birth, but

then he wants me to move back to Tacoma with him,
says I should open a practice there. Can you believe
that someone told him once that Tacoma, Washing-
ton was the home of standard American English?
That is why . . .

A knock at her door made Ruby's cat, Guido, jump down
from her lap, and Ruby stand up with her hands at her kidneys
to support her bulging abdomen and aching back. It would be
her landlord wanting to show the apartment, never mind that
she had asked him to wait until after she was gone.

"Dr. Ruby Gail Okada?" called a voice. "I've got your house
papers!"

Ah, not her landlord. Mr. Utterson's driver, his assistant, or
whatever he was.

"Leave them!" Ruby called.

"Can't. You have to sign where the little arrows point.
Two blue arrows and a red one. The yellow arrow places are
already signed."

"Okay, hold on a second," said Ruby, "I'm not decent."

In terms of what she wore, she was as decent as ever—green
scrubs stolen from the East Village Psychiatric—but in terms
of everything else, as she'd tried to tell Bette, a sense of her
decency had pretty much abandoned her. She smoothed down
the scrubs and opened the door. Mr. Utterson's man stood
gawking. His lips looked like bees had stung them, and he had
the world's worst case of rosacea. His face was also squared
and flattened out by the telltale signatures of Down syndrome.

"Hi there, Gertrude," she said, "I thought Mr. Utterson was
bringing those papers tonight."

"It's Gerard, Dr. Okada. Gertrude is a girl's name."

She squinted at him until his gawk disappeared, replaced by a prideful expression. "Ah, you did this on your own, this signing thing?" she said. "Trying to impress Mr. Utterson?"

"He told me to cease the day. That means take my own initiative."

"Yeah, well, it's *seize*, not *cease*," said Ruby. "It's got a *z* sound at its end, like someone sawing logs. *Cease* means the day is finished, which would be just about all right with me."

She opened her door wide enough for him to see boxes stretched across her apartment floor. "But if you still feel like taking your own initiative, how about helping with these?" she said. "Did you come in Mr. Utterson's car?"

Mr. Utterson, Archie's lawyer, had an old London taxi, which he'd brought to New York when he emigrated from England two decades earlier. The taxi was deep maroon, with white pinstripes along its fenders and doors, swooping into curlicues at its gas tank and headlights. Ruby thought it strange that he paid scrupulous attention to its interior, every detail cherry and original, but had added an aftermarket paint job.

"Parked right outside," Gerard said. "And I know your new house, too, Dr. Okada. It's twenty-something, something, Bank Street, New York, New York, 10014. Mr. Utterson told me to give you the keys after you sign."

"I hope this doesn't mean he's canceling our dinner. I was looking forward to eating something good. I've been surviving on oatmeal and ramen for a week."

"No siree, Bob," Gerard said. "Mr. Utterson said that dinner is on him."

She scanned his face for facetiousness but found only the sincerity that all Down syndrome people seemed to have;

that eternal unwarranted optimism. She walked back over to her laptop, finished, and sent Bette's e-mail—*"Please don't call me, Bette. Let me do my suffering in private."*—and placed the laptop in the last of her boxes. She'd been using a wooden table and chair, made for her by her father as a medical school graduation present. She folded them both, carried them past Gerard and down the half flight of stairs to the vestibule. She'd lived in this apartment for nearly nine years, often saying she would never leave, that rent control was like a steadfast husband.

In the vestibule, she opened her table again, signed Gerard's papers where the arrows pointed, then waited while he traipsed in and out of her apartment, each time carrying two or three boxes. When he came back a final time, she opened her father's chair for him and had him sit down. The boxes weren't heavy, but he was clearly no more suited for this kind of labor than she was. He sat with his knees pressed together and his heels flayed out, his left palm down but his right hand forming the letter *C*, as she saw it.

"Let me get you some water," she said. "I think there's still a glass or two in my cupboard."

She lumbered back into her apartment, found a tumbler with a button at the center of its lid, let the tap run cold, filled the tumbler, wiped it on her scrubs, and, when she carried it back to the vestibule, found Gerard sitting just as she'd left him, with the muscles in his face now doubly flattened out. She hadn't noticed it earlier, but he wore a single black stud earring and had gelled and spiked hair, both of which looked like attachments for a Mr. Potato Head. When Mr. Utterson used the word *catatonia* to describe what occasionally happened to his assistant, she had thought it might be

anything from a focal neurotic lesion to PTSD. But now catatonia seemed right. His belly so severely protruded from his
shirt that two of its buttons wouldn't close. When she shoved
the tumbler into the C of his hand, however, it brought him
back to normal neurological activity. He blinked and put the
tumbler to his lips. Some water ran down his chin.

"Listen, Gerard, how about if I go with you now?" she said.
"If not, I'll have to call a taxi later. I've sworn off using the
subway until after my baby comes."

Her plan had been to take a final walk in Central Park, then
come back for a nap on her braided rug before joining Mr.
Utterson for dinner. But why not get out of here in the light of
day and with somebody? She'd been preparing to go that night
in order to prove that she wasn't afraid, but that now seemed
both foolish and unnecessary.

She went back into her apartment to get her braided rug,
and when she came back this time, Gerard was outside, pacing
by the taxi door, obviously anxious about the change of plans.
He hadn't agreed to take her with him; she had simply foisted
herself upon him.

She smiled and touched his shoulder. "What's your family
name, Gerard?" she asked. "I like to know who I'm talking to,
coming and going."

During all her years of practice, she'd been careful to use
family names, in order to avoid a doctor/patient hierarchy.
If she was to be Dr. Okada, then they would be Mr. or Ms.
so-and-so. And Gerard seemed to appreciate it as much as
her patients did, for now he beamed like the sun had just
come out.

"It's Holbrook, Dr. Okada, like Hal Holbrook!" he said.
"Do you know what Hal is short for?"

"Hmm, maybe Harold?" she said, casting her eyes a little bit skyward.

"It *is* Harold!" he cried. "Harold starts with *H*, and so does Gerard when you say it in Spanish. My mom called me Gerry or Gerrymander, which she said was like a salamander, 'cause it wanders all over the place. I wrote a letter to Hal Holbrook once, but he didn't write back."

"Maybe you ought to try e-mailing him," she said. "You can use my laptop if you want to, once we get to Bank Street. Do you have an e-mail account, Gerard?"

She'd suggested the e-mail to lessen her guilt, but when he said he did have an account and proceeded to recite its address, she looked at the side of the tumbler he still clutched and saw herself reflected there pear shaped and dark.

"I'll find Hal Holbrook's e-mail address for you, then," she said. "How would that be, Gerard?"

3

ONCE SHE WAS IN MR. UTTERSON'S TAXI, a cardboard QUIET! sign silenced Ruby until they got to West Fourth Street near Abingdon Square, where she finally chanced saying, "I think the Bank Street house comes with everything but a place to park."

She feared he might point to the QUIET! sign, but he perked right up.

"Where was my taxi parked just now, Dr. Okada?" he asked. "I mean back by your apartment."

"In front of my building?"

When he turned to face her, he kept his body straight, like Linda Blair in *The Exorcist*. "Mr. Utterson thinks I'm a parking place savant," he said before swinging onto Bank Street and into an open space, as if he'd expected to find it.

The leaves on the parking strip flew up around them in a silent, flat-handed applause. They were directly in front of her new house, which, unlike Mr. Utterson's taxi, had peeling paint, a decrepit exterior, and broken cement steps leading up to its stoop and front door. A cast-iron fence marked a small front yard and the path to the basement. Gerard dug into his pocket for the house keys Mr. Utterson had given him, then got out and carried her father's folding table and chair up to the porch.

"Go in and put everything in the hallway," said Ruby. "And throw me the basement key, would you please, Gerard? I want to check out my new offices."

She waited with her hands out, but he brought the keys back down to her, cradled in his hands like another might cradle water. Throwing was out of the question.

"You take it off the key ring, Dr. Okada," he said. "My fingers are too fat."

She took the key ring, slipped off the basement key, gave him back the others, and carried her medical records down a few steps to a door situated directly beneath the steps going up.

Here, too, she meant to go inside without fanfare, but the door's new slogan flashed at her: *Dr. Ruby G. Okada, General Psychiatry & Medicine*. Damn! It was backward! It was supposed to say *General Medicine and Psychiatry*. But she went in anyway, put her files on a dusty counter, then stepped into each of the basement rooms in turn to open the windows and air the place out. "General psychiatry and medicine," how perfect was that? Could there be a more appropriate receptacle for generalities of the world than psychiatry as she had practiced it?

The back room's windows looked up into a large and

overgrown yard. It was only when she had the thought that the yard would be perfect for Guido to roam around in that she realized she had left him in her apartment! Oh, where was her mind and what further proof did anyone need that she was losing it?

When she ran back outside again, Gerard stood smirking on the sidewalk.

"Hi, Dr. Okada," he said. "Guess who we forgot?"

"I know," she told him. "Guido!"

"No, we forgot your cat! He'll be lonely; We have to go back and get him!"

"He'll not only be lonely, he'll need his medicine soon, too, Gerard. Guido's diabetic."

"Ah," he said. "Your cat is Italian."

Ruby's hope had been to keep Gerard with her until she met Mr. Utterson that night, but now she asked, quite without expecting to, if he thought he could go get Guido without her.

"He's a very nice cat," she said. "Just hold him tightly while you're walking to the car. He won't scratch or bite."

"Here, Guido, here, Guido!" said Gerard. "Coming when you call them is for dogs, isn't it, Dr. Okada? I would like to have a dog sometime."

She thought he would say that he didn't want to lose his parking space, but he simply gave her the rest of the house keys, saying, instead, that he would write his Hal Holbrook e-mail when he got back.

"If I had a dog, I would walk him every day," he said. "At Boys of Summer, they don't allow pets, but they do allow pictures of them. Sometimes a mother pig will let puppies suck her tits. I have a picture of that on my wall."

Some of those applauding leaves were now lodged against

the taxi's windshield. When he picked them off of it, she saw that his fingers were thick and his fingernails flat, with definite signs of clubbing.

"How long has it been since you had a proper physical, Gerard," she asked, "with blood work and a good hard look at everything? A person's blood holds secrets, and I know how to read them. I could do that for you, if you want."

But he put his arms behind him, as if thinking she might pull out a syringe right then, before he had a chance to get her cat.

When he was gone, Ruby went alone into the ground-floor rooms of her new house for the first time, yet without much apprehension. She needed to start living here—since that's what she'd decided to do—and a good way to begin would be to refrigerate Guido's insulin. She pulled it from one of the boxes, tipping its vial until the liquid rose a third of the way up the side. It looked like an encapsulated sea to her, with a ship about to appear on its horizon. *O it's I that am the captain of a tidy little ship / Of a ship that goes a-sailing on the pond . . .* She carried it into the kitchen and placed it in the refrigerator, where it stood like a tidy little lighthouse in the middle of the empty shelves.

Back in the living room, she flipped her braided rug out until its oval cut a pattern on the floor.

There! This room was hers, since she'd claimed it with her rug, which she stood upon now, as if on a braided island.

Looking through the living room window, she could see a child on the steps of the house across the street, waiting for someone to let her in.

4

THE SAFETY OF HER BRAIDED RUG, the only thing she owned that her mother had made for her before she died, allowed Ruby to try to think again in her muddled way just what on earth had moved her to take this house when it was offered to her. But the thoughts were lost again when headlights swept across the living room window and she looked outside and saw that dusk had settled onto Bank Street, and that Gerard's parking space now held a yellow Volkswagen, from which a woman hurried over to let the girl into the house across the street. The woman was late and the girl was angry.

Ruby stood again to go back out into the hallway and open her front door to let a breeze into the house. The stairs to the upper floors of the house were behind her, and across the hall stood a parlor that contained her most prized possessions, sent over two nights earlier. The rest of the house was furnished as it always had been. She opened the parlor door.

Last bits of afternoon light came into the parlor through a line of tall windows. A high and modern desk in the corner seemed made of stainless steel, a de Kooning knockoff hung above a misshapen moss green couch, and a surreal ceramic teapot sat on an emerald coffee table, one drop of tea eternally falling from its spout. Each piece had been made by her father over the years, and sent to her as the spirit grabbed him.

On a silver piano in the center of the room, not made by her father, stood the photo of a man with his hair swept back into a pompadour, in a cross between Elvis and Christopher Walken. Here was her nemesis and benefactor, absent of any of his disguises.

She was about to open this room's windows, too, when

Gerard yelled "Hello!" from the porch. The yellow VW was gone, Mr. Utterson's taxi was back in its space, and Gerard held Guido tightly in his arms.

"Hi there, Guids!" said Ruby. "Welcome to your new home!"

"He was waiting by your other front door, carrying his suitcase, with a feather in his cap," Gerard said. "He's a very nice cat, Dr. Okada. Do you think that Guido likes dogs?"

Ruby ushered them in and closed the front door, but she'd left the parlor door open.

"Hey," said Gerard, "a piano! I can play 'Goodness Gracious' on it!"

"You can?" Ruby asked. "Would you like to play it now? Or would you prefer to write your note to Hal Holbrook?"

"I would prefer to write to Hal!" he said. "Maybe he will answer me if I tell him the story of how we forgot Guido."

"I bet he will," said Ruby. "I think I read somewhere that he appreciates his fans."

Had she read that somewhere, or had she made it up?

When she went in search of her laptop, Gerard stepped to the front of the piano, his earring flashing toward her. He looked about as wide as he was tall. He hit the piano keys four solid times, sang, "You shake my nerves and you rattle my bones!" then hit them four more times.

It's "brain" that you rattle, thought Ruby.

"After you write to Hal, you have to remember to save what you write," she said. "Meanwhile, I will explore the house, if that's okay with you, Gerard."

She brought her laptop into the parlor, opened a blank page for him, then waited while he typed "Dear Mr. Hal Holbrook, I'm Gerard, always called Gerard except by my mother, who used to call me Gerry or Gerrymander. . . ."

He was a *very* fast typist, twice as fast as she was, so she left him to it and went up to the second-floor landing before stopping to look down over the banister. Both the living room and parlor doors were open now, giving the floor between them a grid of overlapping light. When she said aloud, "I wonder where I'll sleep tonight?" Guido came out of the parlor and began climbing up to her with difficulty. She hadn't thought that at his age he mightn't be able to handle a three-story house. When he got to her, she picked him up and carried him into the second-floor bedroom with her, which had windows looking over the backyard. In front of one of them stood a telescope beside an easy chair and ottoman. The room was built for reading and spying, or reading and looking at the stars. When she leaned down to examine the telescope, she put Guido on the ottoman.

"Should I turn these knobs?" she asked him. "Put things into focus for us?"

She feared that what would *never* be in focus for her was how she had agreed to take, from a sick and fractured man, an entire furnished house. She picked Guido up again and put his eye to the telescope. He didn't like to be manhandled, but this time his body grew still and his eyes grew round. She rubbed her cheek against him in order to feel his softness, and to listen to the crazy beating of his heart. Before Bob came into her life, she had talked to Guido constantly; after Bob, hardly at all.

A small metal plate affixed to the middle of the telescope had one arrow pointing up and another pointing down. She pushed the up arrow and watched the telescope slide along its shaft.

"Hey, Guids, look at this," she said, but Guido had slipped out of her arms to trundle across the room and sit in the corner with a paw up, like one of those ceramic cats she used to see in Japanese restaurants.

Chapter Two

5

RUBY HADN'T BEEN THERE in a while, but when Mr. Utterson had suggested that they meet at Il Buco, she'd nearly asked him to pick another restaurant. She'd eaten there a few times before with Bette and believed it would be too crowded for the kind of conversation they needed to have, and perhaps give too much air to her own barely hidden derangements. But to have suggested another restaurant might have used up her small amount of veto power, which she feared she might need later on.

When Gerard, who was driving her, turned onto Bond Street, a parking space came open directly in front of the restaurant. A queue of people waiting for tables looked at her when she got out of his taxi, then past her at Gerard, who stayed where he was.

Mr. Utterson stood at the bar, tossing down the remnants of a tumbler of gin. When he saw her, he pointed at a glass of wine he'd also bought, then said, "Yes, of course, how silly of me" when she gestured at her abdomen.

Their table was in a corner directly to the right of the front door.

While Ruby wriggled out of her scarf and coat and wedged

her body into a chair, Mr. Utterson pulled a large manila envelope from his briefcase, straightened its creases, then sat down himself. A thin forest of hair stood at the front of his head, and deep lines sliced quarter moons on either side of his mouth, making it seem as though he was about to say something parenthetical.

His was a view of the restaurant's interior, hers (through a window) of the people waiting by Gerard's parked car. Mr. Utterson asked when her baby was due, just as a waitress came over to say her name was Ashley and that the chowder and osso buco were finished for the night.

"October thirty-first," said Ruby. "Scariest day of the year. I hope he's born before sundown."

"So you know it's a he," Mr. Utterson said. "I remember the days when we were surprised by what came out."

"I'd give some serious thought to the lamb or clam risotto," Ashley said. "The crispy duck's good, too, but order the sauce on the side."

Ruby ordered spaghetti, plus a salad with anchovies.

"And El Diablo?" Ashley asked. "You look like a lamb man to me."

"*Quaglia, carne cruda*, and another Malbec," said Mr. Utterson.

He had nearly finished the wine he'd bought for Ruby, but had Ashley really called him El Diablo? Ruby believed that the true devil of the evening was the deed to the Bank Street house, which sat inside that manila envelope.

"I know this is all confusing," Mr. Utterson said when they were alone. "I've been in this business since Thatcher and Reagan, nearly, and I've never seen anything like it."

He patted the envelope. "I don't mean the legalities; the

legalities are fine, and your look tells me that I should stick to them, not poke my nose in where it doesn't belong."

"You're not poking your nose in; I just didn't like that waitress," said Ruby. "And for the record, you don't look like a lamb man. You look like a man who wants two appetizers and another Malbec."

When he smiled, the skin beside his eyes crinkled up. She looked at an antique coffee grinder on the nearby window ledge, a 1950s-era juicer by its side. There were other such knickknacks everywhere around the restaurant, diners hunched below them like time travelers.

"I suppose in psychiatry you meet men like him every day," he said, "but if I'm really not intruding, may I ask whether you still use words like *crazy*? Not to sound clumsy or idiotic about it, but I often find myself wishing that we didn't define human ailments quite so narrowly as we do. No, I don't mean our 'ailments'; I mean our eccentricities. Why can't we just let people be?"

"We still use all the old standbys—*crazy, loony, nuttier than a fruitcake*—but we try not to do so in front of our patients," Ruby told him.

She smiled a little grimly, sighed, and said, "Look, Mr. Utterson, it's been a long and trying day for me. First I forgot my cat, and I just realized now that I have forgotten your papers."

The papers were in the living room, atop the box that had held Guido's insulin.

"If the papers are the reason for our meal, shouldn't we call it a night?" she said. "I'm as tired as a woman can be . . . tired of body and of spirit."

She had not remotely meant to say that. She'd meant to sit

there for an hour, smiling across the table at him and having something good to eat.

Mr. Utterson paused, his hands on the envelope in front of him, his feelings clearly hurt.

"Tomorrow will do for the papers," he said. "Of course, had you brought them tonight, I would have given you the deed to the ranch, as it were, and concluded our business. I *had* hoped to gain an understanding of him, but you're right; it's none of my business."

Poke his nose in? None of his business? Here was a man who took the blame for things immediately. Who couldn't use a man like that?

She was glad, however, that tomorrow would do as well as tonight for the papers. She'd worried he might send Gerard for them, and she wanted him stationed outside, ready to take her home should she truly decide to call it a night. She smiled and said that Gerard had helped her greatly, that he *did* look like a lamb man, and that maybe they should order him some and send it out.

"Gerard packs his own dinner," Mr. Utterson said. "Not 'packs' like one would put a dinner together at home. I simply mean he gets it from a little gourmet deli I introduced him to. He has his breakfast there, too. I don't actually pay Gerard, Dr. Okada, but I do get him various gifts, buy him his meals, try to make his days a little easier."

That made Ruby suspicious again. Why not simply pay the man if he wanted to make his days a little easier? But her job here and now, or, for that matter, anywhere anymore, was not to judge how others lived their lives. Her job was to have her baby and get on with living her own. She thought of her father, the exemplar of that, thinking straight and looking clearly and taking the simplest path.

"I agree that we sometimes define eccentricities too narrowly," she said. "What people call crazy, even what some psychiatrists do, is often not much more than our failure to understand the spectacular breadth and depth of normality. In my experience, anyway, it's not uncommon for a person to get convinced of his own craziness, when all he has to do is accept himself. Or *her*self, as the case may be."

"But not our Archie Billingsly, right? You're not talking about his level of craziness, certainly."

She looked out the window at the taxi, where Gerard sat eating his deli dinner by himself. Mr. Utterson was good at drawing her out, but this was delving way too deeply into what she'd promised herself she would avoid. She thought of the strong, clear lines of her father's table and chair and willed herself to have their strength.

When Ashley brought Mr. Utterson's Malbec, one of his appetizers, and her anchovy salad and spaghetti, she speared an anchovy on a single tine of her fork, then reached across the table to tap the envelope.

"How can I carry on about the spectacular depth and breadth of normality like I did just now, then automatically exclude him?" she asked. "The truth is, I don't know, but you seem to have concluded he was sane enough to give me his house."

She could feel the anchovy bones breaking in her mouth, but Mr. Utterson only shrugged. "I met him just twice," he said, "but craziness and the law, strange to say, often make comfortable bedfellows."

He halved his quail down the middle. Though he had spoken firmly, it made it look as if he were of two minds.

"Okay, fair enough, but let me ask it clearly so I'm sure I haven't missed anything," she said. "Once I give you those papers, no one can undo things later on, is that correct?"

"In a nutshell, yes," he said.

His smile expanded the quarter-moon creases around his mouth. In a movie, Jack Nicholson would play him. It made her ease up.

"Okay, then, why did you ask me to dinner tonight if tomorrow is fine for the papers?" she asked. "Surely not merely to make jokes about nutshells and such."

Mr. Utterson ran a finger around the rim of his wineglass until a gloomy musical note rang out into the room.

"As I've said, to satisfy my curiosity," he told her. "It's unprofessional of me, maybe, but I didn't want to move back to London without having a clearer idea of the man."

Ruby lowered her eyes. If he moved back to London, what would happen to Gerard?

"Well then, here it is in your nutshell," she said. "Some psychiatrists would say right away he has a dissociative disorder, rare as that is, but others, myself included, think it's something else—for lack of better words, a psychotic episode not otherwise specified, which is what I just tried to tell you."

That sounded trivial even to her.

"That's a bit like my mechanic telling me 'There's something wrong with your car but we don't know what it is,'" he said.

Ruby spiked another anchovy. Her craving for salt was extraordinary.

"In many ways, psychiatry is precisely that general," she said. "Freud only died in 1939, you know, and until the late Fifties it was bedlam, bedlam, bedlam all over the place. The human brain is the last frontier, Mr. Utterson, and we are only at the outskirts of it. And you and I both know, I think, that we are also only at the outskirts of whatever is ailing Archie B. Billingsly."

That felt a bit more satisfying. It meant that a psychotic episode could be trivial, something inside the breath and depth of normality, but could also be about as rare as the atmosphere on distant stars.

"So before Freud, we might have been talking about possession?" Mr. Utterson asked.

He had finished both his appetizers and was eyeing Ruby's spaghetti, as yet hardly touched. When Ashley came to ask how everything was, Ruby ordered cheesecake. She pushed her spaghetti away.

"Make it two," said Mr. Utterson, "plus one more wine for El Diablo."

"Well, possession is what they called it in the nineteenth century," Ruby said. "What we seem to be doing now is searching for a more sophisticated terminology. . . ." And then she quite unexpectedly asked, "Have you told Gerard that you're moving back to London? And are you taking him with you? He'd be lost without you, you know. . . ."

His new wine came instantly, along with the two pieces of cheesecake, but Ruby no longer wanted that, either. She wanted to go home.

"With Gerard, a long lead time doesn't yield many benefits," Mr. Utterson said. "And how could I take him with me? He's a man who needs to keep the life he's got, and I will see to that before I go."

He looked at her fiercely now, like Jack Nicholson in *The Shining*.

"Do you know what they call Gerard's brand of Down syndrome?" he asked. "They call it 'mosaic.' Isn't that beautiful? It makes me think that he's made up entirely of art."

When she saw that it embarrassed him to say such a thing, she was moved to stay a little while longer in the restaurant.

"It *is* beautiful," she said. "It's as if he were dropped and shattered, then put back together again. But okay, if you forced me to label *his* condition—I mean Archie Billingsly's now—I would use an art term, too. I'd call it a fugue. It's as if he rode off on one kind of horse and came back on a horse of an entirely different color. My father would have called it 'tripping,' hippie that he was."

To her astonishment, tears rolled into Mr. Utterson's eyes.

"Mosaic and fugue! Two ways for artists to look at human frailty!" he said.

He leaned across the table, his drunkenness showing.

"Do you know why he hired me? Do you know why, of all the lawyers in New York City, this unbelievable fellow chose me?"

"Haven't a clue," she said. "Looked you up online?"

"He chose me because of my name! I'm the only attorney named Utterson in all of New York City. He told me he had an uncle by that name, whom he admired!"

She *knew* she'd heard his name before, and snapped her fingers.

"You weren't his uncle; you were his invention!" she said. "Or I should say you were Bob's. He chose you because the other Mr. Utterson was trustworthy."

Ah, but this had gone on long enough. She didn't like drunks.

She pushed her chair back and stood. She intended to go to

the ladies' room but opened the restaurant's front door instead and went out onto the street. The taxi was where he'd parked it, but Gerard stood inside the small fenced entryway, talking with a trio of pretty young women.

"I bet he will write you back," one of them said. "If I got a letter from a guy like you, I'd ask him out to dinner. Maybe right here at Il Buco."

"Hi there, Gerrymander," said Ruby. She nodded at the Tupperware box under his arm and asked him how his dinner was.

"I had quiche Lorraine, Dr. Okada," Gerard said. "But my friends here are saying that it gives me bad breath."

"Yeah?" said Ruby. "Which friend said that?"

He pointed at the tallest young woman. "Cotton-tail said it," he said.

"Good evening, Cotton-tail," said Ruby. "On the lookout for a bit of cheap fun?"

"What's it to you?" asked Cotton-tail. "He the father of your child?"

Just then, Il Buco's door opened again and Mr. Utterson came out.

"Ah," said Cotton-tail, "my mistake. Here's your baby daddy now."

"Good night, Flopsy and Mopsy!" said Gerard. "Good night, Cotton-tail!"

Mr. Utterson laughed, ready to tell them that they were in the presence of a man made up entirely of art, but what Ruby wanted more than anything just then was to go find Farmer McGregor's rifle, so she could take careful aim and blow them all to hell.

Chapter Three

6

R UBY SLEPT BADLY, WAKING OFTEN, until she heard the old rock song "Morning Has Broken," wafting through her bedroom window at just after 6:00 A.M. She looked at Guido beside her on the bed. "That's Cat Stevens, Guids," she said. "You should probably like him, since you're a cat, too."

These days, she often noticed that music was mostly hidden in tiny storage devices, and mainlined into people's heads through earplugs, but she liked the idea of sharing a song with the neighbors, and that brought her back to *fugue* again, and then to *mosaic*.

She sat up with a strong premonition that "Moonshadow" would be next, though she knew it wasn't next on the album. She picked up a book she'd brought upstairs with her the night before, dog-eared and thin, like the copy of *The Waste Land* that she'd also read in her tree house, "April is the cruelest month" pretty much defining the kind of kid she was. Now, however, what she read so engaged her that she failed to notice "Moonshadow" when it did come on.

> *Mr. Utterson the lawyer was a man of rugged countenance, that was never lighted by a smile; cold, scanty and embarrassed in discourse; backward in*

sentiment; lean, long, dusty, dreary, and yet somehow lovable. At friendly meetings, and when the wine was to his taste, something eminently human beaconed from his eye; something indeed which never found its way into his talk, but which spoke not only in these silent symbols of the after-dinner face, but more often and loudly in the acts of his life. He was austere with himself; drank gin when he was alone, to mortify a taste for vintages; and though he enjoyed the theatre, had not crossed the doors of one for twenty years. But he had an approved tolerance for others; sometimes wondering, almost with envy, at the high pressure of spirits involved in their misdeeds; and in any extremity inclined to help rather than to reprove. "I incline to Cain's heresy," he used to say quaintly: "I let my brother go to the devil in his own way."

Her Mr. Utterson was drinking gin when she first saw him, but it hadn't mortified his taste for vintages. That something eminently human beckoned from his eye was undeniable, since tears soon followed.

She put the book down and went to the window and opened it and stuck her head out into the morning, like Scrooge after his third ghost's Christmas visit. "Moonshadow" came roaring in at full volume.

She ducked back in again in order to try to train the telescope on the sound. At first there was nothing, but soon she flitted it past a boom box sitting on a picnic table, a man stretched out beside it. She went past him several more times before she was able to steady the telescope. He wore a plain gray sweatshirt, with a jacket folded beneath a mop of dark brown hair, his eyes focused upward on the rain clouds. She shifted the telescope toward a swatch of visible belly, but when she tried to shift it back to his face again, she lost him.

She pushed the telescope away, getting out of her bedroom as fast as she could, to run downstairs and fling herself around the ground-floor banister and along the hallway to the kitchen, where she banged the back door open before stopping as suddenly as she'd started. What was she doing? She was barefoot and pregnant and still in her pajamas, her abdomen plowing the air in front of her like the prow of that infamous little ship.

She sat at the kitchen table with her head in her hands, but after only a minute's worth of outright grief, she stood again to open the refrigerator and look in at Guido's insulin box, still sitting where she'd put it.

What beacon was it, blinking from her subconscious mind, that had made her take this house from him? Sometimes she glimpsed it, but mostly it left her in darkness, and made her feel bereft.

She picked up the insulin box and rattled the vial within it until Guido trotted into the kitchen.

$$7$$

WHEN THE DOORBELL RANG at 3:00 P.M., Ruby was upstairs, hanging the last of her clothing. She went to the second-floor landing to call down "Hold your horses, Geronimo!" and when Gerard called back, "Horses held!" she stepped into the bathroom to look at herself in the full-length mirror behind its door. She was pretty, like her mother had been, pretty in the way of a one-half-Asian Audrey Hepburn, but she'd be forty soon, too old to run into her wild backyard in her pajamas, or to want to kill a bitch named Cotton-tail.

The first few times she went up and down the stairs, Guido had faithfully followed her, but when she turned at the bend in the stairway now, she saw him sitting by the front door, waiting for Gerard, who peered through the glass on the door's right side, its bevel abstracting him mightily.

"Guess what, Dr. Okada," he said. "Mr. Utterson might take me to England with him, and his Labor Day gift to me is Hal Holbrook's e-mail address, so you don't have to find it now!"

The moment she opened the door, she understood that it hadn't been only the window's bevel that abstracted him, for he also wore a big white suit, and a big white wig on his head.

"It's the Mark Twain outfit Mr. Utterson gave me last Christmas!" he said.

When Ruby laughed, Gerard laughed, too, but then asked, "What's so funny, Dr. Okada?"

"I'm just marveling at life," she said. "It does have its surprises, don't you think?"

"I will ask Hal in my e-mail to him!" he said. "If I ask him a serious question, maybe he'll write me back."

He looked into the parlor, where her laptop still sat, open and waiting for him since the last time he'd used it.

"Do you want to go to England with Mr. Utterson?" Ruby asked. "If you do, I'll miss you, Gerard."

"I'll ask Hal whether I should go to England and whether life has its surprises! Two good questions might make him want to tell me what to do."

"Okay, while you do that, I'll keep putting things away," Ruby said, but Gerard had already gone in and gotten to work.

Ruby had noticed when she was getting that book the night before that a door stood at the back of the living room, blocked by one of its bookcases. When she opened her practice, she would need a way to get downstairs without having to go outside, but could she remove this bookcase, even get rid of its books, without taking the time to look at them?

The books on the bookcase in question all had authors whose names began with *M*. *Island,* by MacLeod, next to *Paris 1919,* by MacMillan, next to *Moby-Dick.* She had just begun to pull them down and stack them, never mind the insult, when Gerard came in from the parlor. Not five minutes had passed, but he was taking a break from his e-mail. When he saw *Island,* he asked if he could have it, since Mr. Utterson often told him that no man was one.

"Take any book you like," she said, "but help me get them out of here, okay? We can use some of the boxes I just unpacked."

Gerard stuck *Island* down his pants, collected the empty boxes from the porch, removed the rest of the books, then pushed the bookcase away and freed the door.

"Look," said Ruby, "the doorknob's missing. How are we going to open it? You don't have a tool kit in your car, do you, Gerard?"

He said he did have a tool kit, but also pulled a screwdriver from a pocket of his Mark Twain suit, where he'd kept it, he said, since Mr. Utterson told him he had a screw loose. When he stuck it in the doorknob hole and levered it up, the door creaked far enough open for a rectangle of darkness to appear. Ruby stuck her fingers in to feel the inside wall, but she couldn't find a light switch.

"I have a torch in the taxi!" Gerard said. "Do you know

what *torch* means in American English, Dr. Okada? *Torch* means 'flashlight'!"

He was out the door fast and back in a minute with the torch, not nearly as exhausted as he had been yesterday. Ruby, meanwhile, had pulled the door open wide and placed a foot down on the uppermost step. She asked Gerard to keep his torch beam in front of her, but he ran it up the walls to a line of framed photographs that flicked in and out of its light. To their right were pictures of women; to their left were photos of men. The woman at the top of the stairs stood on what appeared to be the stoop of this very house. On a square of paper beneath the photo were the words *Anna Stevenson Billingsly, 1932*. Across the stairway from her hung Archie *S.* Billingsly (1925–1944). He wore a Marine Corps uniform, so perhaps he'd been killed in World War II.

"I think we've found the rogues gallery here," said Ruby. "The primary suspects all lined up."

To her surprise, the second photo on the right was also of Anna Stevenson Billingsly, in 1968, this time pretending to write a letter at a secretary desk. Across from her stood Archie *O.* Billingsly, 1944–1980. He had long and tangled hair and wore a light blue work shirt . . . had obviously either been a hippie or a fellow traveler.

Photo number three, Anna Stevenson Billingsly again, was labeled with the inclusive dates 1894–1996, so she had lived to be 102 years old. Across from her there was no young man this time, but a picture labeled *Bell Rock Lighthouse*, brilliantly lit in a ferocious storm. Old Anna's hair seemed to blow around her face, as if in the wind from that very storm.

Ruby asked Gerard to train the torch on the door at the

bottom of the stairs. To her relief, it had a doorknob, plus Guido sitting there waiting for them.

When Gerard flashed the torch into the face in the final picture on the wall's right side, they found a painting labeled *Robert Stevenson, Lighthouse Engineer (1772–1850)*.

"Dr. Okada!" said Gerard. "The women have someone to look at, but not this old guy."

Something *had* hung across from Robert Stevenson, for they could see its outline and a hook on the wall. Ruby took the torch and cast its beam upon the stormy Bell Rock Lighthouse. It was equal in size to the outlined space across from Robert Stevenson, and bulged away from the wall in an awkward way.

"Go get that one for me," she said. "I think it belongs down here."

Ruby feared it would be hard for Gerard to lift the painting, but, in fact, it came away from the wall quite easily.

"Hey!" he said, "there's someone else behind it, another young guy!"

"Leave it but bring me the lighthouse," said Ruby. "If you can hold on to it for another few seconds, I'll try to hook it to its original place on the wall."

The frame had a horizontal wire stretched across its back, bent where a hook was supposed to reside. She put her thumb on the wire, her middle finger on the wall hook, then guided the wire down until her thumb met her finger and the frame settled back into place. She slid her arm out and flicked the torch to where the lighthouse had hung before, to find Archie B. Billingsly looking at her, young, like the other two Archies, with his hair swept back.

She imagined a boom box just outside the camera's range.

8

The basement looked like it had when she brought in her medical files, but the door leading to the backyard wasn't latched, as it surely had been before.

"Get that last woman for me, will you please, Gerard?" said Ruby. "I mean the one he was across from."

She held up Archie B. Billingsly's picture when she said 'he,' the one she had taken from the wall herself, then pushed open the unlatched door and walked up the stairs to the backyard. The fence to her left was high, but a line of trees overcame the sense that there was any fence at all. She simply felt like she was entering a wilderness.

She waited for Gerard to join her, the oldest version of Anna Stevenson Billingsly cradled in his arms.

"This morning I saw him from my window," she said. "He was back there listening to music, or maybe playing music for me, I don't know."

She held up Archie's picture again, the third in a line of Archie Billingslys, each with a different middle name.

"Why don't we go ask him?" said Gerard. "Mr. Utterson always says that asking people things is the best way to find them out!"

His Mark Twain wig gaped up on his head, a bit like a second mouth.

To their left, a narrow path led into the overgrowth. Once, during her surgery rotation in Seattle, Ruby had observed the lung transplant of a woman with otherwise-terminal cystic fibrosis. When the woman's old lungs were set aside, they looked to Ruby like a brain laced heavily with schizophrenia. Never mind that schizophrenia couldn't be observed that way or that lungs did not resemble a brain, it was what had decided her on psychiatry, and now, as she stepped onto the path, she got the feeling they were stepping into that woman's castaway lungs.

"We shouldn't go far," she told Gerard.

She knew that her backyard couldn't be deeper than others on the block, but the sense that they could walk forever overwhelmed her.

"I feel like no one's been here in years," she said, "but I saw him just a few hours ago."

"Let's count our steps, and if we don't find him in thirty paces, we'll go back," Gerard said. "That's ten more paces than in an old-time duel, Dr. Okada!"

She looked at Archie B. Billingsly's photo again, the man seemingly unencumbered by illness, his future stretching brightly before him. Was that why he'd hidden it behind the lighthouse . . . to say that his future was dark now?

They started their thirty paces right away but soon lost count. Ruby feared that the path would narrow even more, igniting her childhood claustrophobia, when suddenly they did reach the clearing, complete with the picnic table that she'd seen from her bedroom window.

Gerard went to the clearing's far edge, where the path meandered on.

When Ruby put her fingers on the table's wood, she found that it was soft, that it felt like touching moss. But this was where he'd lain; she could nearly see his outline in the wood's soft crust.

"From here the path goes up!" Gerard said, but she was sure that wasn't true, and she didn't feel like climbing into anyone else's imagination.

When Gerard disappeared along it, she asked him to wait for her, but the only answer she got was from a pair of nearby mockingbirds, pretending to be something else.

"Don't go too far!" Ruby called. "Gerard, where are you?"

"He says he wants some cheese," Gerard said. "He says that cheese is what he misses most."

"Who says that? Who wants cheese?" shouted Ruby.

She was suddenly angry, and knew it was reflected in her voice. When she came in sight of him, Gerard had his jacket slung over his shoulder.

"The man who was just here," he said. "He told me he's been eating berries and oysters for three long years, and he'd really like some cheese, if we have any. I told him I don't like cheese, Dr. Okada."

"Okay, if there was a man here, what did he look like?" Ruby hissed. "This is not the time for making things up, Gerard."

She tried to find a second path that a man could have run down, but there were no other paths, only this one.

"Okay, let's go back," she said. "Let's get your e-mail done. How does that sound, Gerard?"

She meant it as an apology for letting him see her anger.

"But I do like the cheese of toasted cheese sandwiches," Gerard said.

From that, she learned that food meant more than words, that apologies had to be tactile.

Chapter Four

9

DURING THE REST OF HER FIRST WEEK in the Bank Street house, Ruby cleaned each room twice, and bought what she needed in order to begin her new life—more syringes and a sack of Purina DM cat food for Guido, proper fresh fruits and vegetables for a pregnant woman, and basic supplies for her clinic.

During her second week, when living in Archie's house no longer seemed like such a lie to her, she hired men to rewire and repaint the basement, at a cost of about triple what she'd expected. Still, she kept busy, imposing on herself these rules: (1) stay away from the telescope; (2) don't go into that backyard; and (3) try not to think too much about anything.

To go with her three rules, her clinic had three rooms, if she didn't count the reception area. One she would use for seeing patients, another would become her private office, and she offered the third—the only room with an adjoining bathroom—to Gerard to live in, on the condition that he act as her receptionist until she got herself together enough to hire someone. She said she couldn't pay him but that he could fulfill his lifelong dream of getting a dog, if the dog didn't terrorize Guido or bark too much. She knew he was considering going to England with Mr. Utterson but hoped he would not, hoped that a dog might keep him next to her, at least until her baby came.

All these new possibilities turned Gerard somewhat frantic, but he did move into the room, complete with his bed and his poster of a sow suckling puppies. What's more, he hung four of the stairwell pictures in the newly painted offices. Old Robert Stevenson greeted anyone who came through the door, and the various versions of Anna Stevenson Billingsly hung here and there—young, middle-aged, and ancient. Ruby wouldn't allow him to hang the Archie photos, so they graced the bottoms of various drawers.

Gerard still drove for Mr. Utterson, of course, leaving Ruby alone most evenings to sit and read, or sit and listen to music with Guido. She initially thought that being alone in the house would frighten her, but she loved the CDs her father had sent her, currently something called *Blue Miles*, which she listened to while sipping the daily half ounce of whiskey that Dr. Muir, her OB-GYN, quite atypically allowed her.

"A half ounce a day will give my grandson an artistic temperament; it will make him fluid when I teach him how to draw," her father had said when she told him.

She liked *Blue Miles* because it was far away from "Moonshadow"; much more akin to the isolated highway she was on. Blue miles to go before I sleep was how she thought of it.

Perhaps the old jazz made her seek older reading material also, for soon enough she found herself eschewing her professional journals in favor of ancient descriptions of the oddest-possible variants of the human personality. She reread parts of Silvano Arieti's, *Interpretation of Schizophrenia* from 1955, but most particularly Arturo Pentimonti's *Lament for Others*, a 1920s pamphlet that described an empathy of such depth and clarity that when possessed by it, the patient *became* the lamented one, traveling with him either down through the circles of a terrible psychotic hell or up into the clear blue skies of a visionary euphoria.

The pamphlet recounted a nineteenth-century Russian composer in such grave despair over Mozart's death at thirty-five that as he passed his own thirty-fifth birthday he began to feel the great man's presence—Mozart's hand on his as he wrote his greatest scores. His fame grew, the concert halls filled, until he was cured by none other than Grigory Rasputin, and spent the rest of his life with Mozart nowhere near him, and unable to compose.

Her father had found the pamphlet in a antiquarian bookstore in Tacoma, and given it to her upon her medical school graduation.

His inscription read "For my daughter when she forgets herself."

10

A COUPLE OF DAYS INTO HER THIRD WEEK in the house, when music once more woke her, Ruby thought, No, not again!

This time, however, it was only her phone tweeting out its melody from the table beside her bed. Her clinic's grand opening was to be that day, but she'd intended to sleep in, to open it after lunch, not now. She'd ignored her father's suggestion that she open her clinic after her baby was born, never mind that it was far more logical.

She picked up her phone, stretching the word *Yesss?* out, her irritation hidden beneath her pillow.

"Hi, Dr. Okada! Guess who I'm with!" said Gerard.

"I don't know, Hal Holbrook? Didn't I tell you noon, Gerard?"

"No, not Mr. Holbrook. That would be silly! And anyway, it's a she I'm with, Dr. Okada! Who I'm with is a girl!"

God, thought Ruby, not Bette.

She carried her phone to the window by the telescope to look out at the trees and foliage.

"Is she middle-aged and wrinkled and scheming about her career?"

"Ha-ha, Dr. Okada. How can a dog do that?"

"Gerard! I thought our deal was that Guido would get a vote! And don't we have enough to do today? You're jumping the gun by a mile!"

Gerard was quiet for so long that she started picking up yesterday's clothing. Guido was on her bed, his paws in the air and his mouth open.

"Okay," she finally said. "How big is she and where did you get her and is she housebroken yet?"

"Mr. Utterson bought her for me when I told him I wouldn't go to England with him. If you take a dog to England, she has to go to jail for six months, Dr. Okada, and Francesca's not yet six months old!"

"Francesca, Gerard? You didn't get a poodle, I hope."

All of Ruby's pregnancy clothes were stretched and worn.

"She's a bulldog, but she'll only grow as big as a loaf of French bread. Thick French bread, though, not a baguette, Mr. Utterson says."

Ruby was sure that Mr. Utterson had bought that dog so he wouldn't have to take Gerard to England, yet down in her clinic a half an hour later, who should show up with Gerard and Francesca but Mr. Utterson himself, bundles of flowers falling from his arms. Ruby hadn't seen him since the night of their dinner, and he looked a little better in the daylight. He seemed to have more hair, and he was thinner than she'd supposed, even slightly muscular.

Gerard wore dark green corduroy pants and a bloodred sweater with reindeers embossed upon it.

"Look how cute Francesca is!" he said. "Bulldogs have funny faces, don't they, Dr. Okada? Mr. Utterson says that she looks like Edward W. Robinson."

"Edward *G.* Robinson," Mr. Utterson said while Francesca waddled across the room to sit at Ruby's feet, Edward G. Robinson in the flesh.

Did middle initials define who someone was?

When Ruby spotted Guido on top of the file cabinet, she picked Francesca up and carried her over to introduce her to her cat. She could feel Francesca's ribs and thudding heartbeat, and she could hear Guido's hiss.

Neither animal looked at the other, but both sets of ears fell back and both sets of noses sniffed.

11

AT JUST BEFORE NOON, dressed in a pressed white medical jacket and wearing a pair of new black stretch pants, Ruby strolled around her clinic to make sure things were in order, that they hadn't been put out of order by the sudden addition of Francesca to the weird little family she had formed. Guido had a basket by the door, but whenever she put him in it, he jumped back out. And Francesca simply followed Guido wherever he went.

"How about we think of having them down here as an experiment, Gerard," said Ruby. "Sometimes experiments work and sometimes they . . ."

She waited for him to say "don't," but he said instead, "And sometimes a placebo works just as well, Dr. Okada. A placebo is a medicine that pretends."

At noon exactly, the very minute of her official clinic opening, and with Mr. Utterson out buying them lunch, the telephone rang from its spot on Gerard's reception desk. Part of his job was to answer the phone, so Ruby waited to see if he'd use the words she'd told him to use. He looked at the phone at ring one, put a hand on it at ring two, and picked it up just as the third ring ended.

"You have reached the offices of Dr. Ruby G. Okada," he said. "We can't take your call right now, but please leave a message after the beep."

He used a falsetto British accent, and the beep his voice made a few seconds later sounded outright metallic. He stuck the receiver in the crook of his neck and picked up a notepad and pencil from his desk. Ruby waited until he finished writing his note and brought it over to her. If she said what she wanted to say—that Gerard had to *answer* the phone, not pretend a machine was doing it—she'd be late for her only patient of the day, who'd be arriving at any minute. Still, she stared at him hard, hoping he would see her displeasure, before finally reading the note, which surprised her twice—first by the beauty of Gerard's handwriting, and second because the message was from Bette.

She nearly asked if she could listen to the message herself. Gerard, however, had hung his head.

"Mr. Utterson likes it when I do it like that," he said. "He says it gives him a tactical advantage."

"But we don't want a tactical advantage. We want patients."

That Bette was not a patient, he didn't point out.

Since Ruby's arrival at Bank Street, Bette had called a few times, but Ruby had neither picked up her phone nor called Bette back. The note said "What did you do, Rubescence, hire an Englishman to answer your phone? In any case, I'm calling to wish you luck. Break a leg, or whatever it is they say. . . . And call me fucking back, okay?"

Gerard had pressed down hard on the expletive.

Ruby was about to apologize again, to ask him gently to simply answer the phone next time, when the basement door opened and a woman walked in. So instead of saying anything, she took up the file Gerard had prepared and pretended to study it. *Mary Andrew Michaelsonsen* said its label, but the file itself was empty. The woman wore a light gray skirt, a trim white shirt, and carried a dark gray cap. It seemed that Ruby's first patient was a nun.

"Hi, come in!" she said. "It's an auspicious day for us!"

"So Gerard said," replied the woman. "He tells me what goes on."

Gerard tells her what goes on? Had he done so when she called to make her appointment?

She was younger than Ruby, with a well-scrubbed face, and she wore a pair of pretty blue Keds. Ruby ushered her into her private office and asked her to sit down. Some of Mr. Utterson's flowers were on her desk, obscuring her view of Mary Andrew Michael*son* or Michael*sen,* whichever the case.

"Is it Sister Mary Andrew, then?" asked Ruby.

"I guess you can say that I'm a semi-sister," said the woman, "but I'm here because I can't sleep. I go to sleep easily enough after a day of hard work at the soup kitchen, but then I wake up later and ask myself, How can this go on?"

Ah, a soup kitchen! Before his deli days, Gerard used to eat at one.

"It's a pretty good question. Did you come up with any answers?" Ruby asked.

The woman pulled on a tuft of wayward brown hair, then rested her chin on her palms. Her file had a pencil attached to it, but its string was so short that when Ruby tried to write, the file started nodding at the seminun.

"I slept well until recently," she said, "but now, but now . . ."

In the old days, Ruby would have fixed this woman's sleeplessness pharmacologically, and in a single visit. But she felt the urge to hear the woman talk, so she asked her what was hard about working in a soup kitchen.

"What's hard about it? *What's hard about it?* Have you ever worked in one? Have you ever spent time tending to the needs of the down-and-out, and not asking too many questions?"

Her incredulity reminded Ruby of her own a moment earlier, when Gerard had pretended to be an answering machine.

"No, I haven't, but questions are the tools of my trade," said Ruby. "Like yours, I presume, is compassion."

Now the woman shrugged. ""I guess from the outside it might look like that," she said, "but most of the time we simply serve people food and try not to judge."

"Well, what is that if not compassion?"

Ruby thought it was a pretty good question, but Mary Andrew Michaelsonsen didn't seem to hear it.

"Week after week there are so many of them!" she said. "Just this morning I served three hundred people. And it's not just soup, either, but bacon and eggs. . . . Once a farmer from upstate gave us ten thousand breakfast steaks, for crying out loud!"

Now it was Ruby's turn to shrug.

"You're lucky to have a job where you can count your successes," she said. "Three hundred people eating breakfast means three hundred people who won't go hungry for a while."

She hadn't thought she would be—it hadn't been that long—but she was out of practice. It wasn't her job, in the first five minutes, to tell a new patient to get over herself.

"You get to know a lot of strange people at a soup kitchen. Some you know by name; others want to tell you their stories. . . . But the thing of it is, though you get to know them, they never take the time to know you. They're a self-centered bunch, the homeless."

Ruby tried to free her short-leashed pencil, and in the process broke its lead. She found a pen in her desk and wrote "The homeless are a self-centered bunch" on the file's first page. Seeing it there made her smile.

"You may think it's funny, but it's me, me, me all the livelong day with the homeless. Not once in a month does anyone even ask you how you slept!"

"I would think that thoughtlessness among the homeless probably hasn't changed much over the years," Ruby said. "Come on now, tell me what's happened lately to cause your lack of sleep. Let's try to work this out."

"Well, one man has been an exception recently, wanting to know how I am and waiting for my reply. . . . It's he who's been screwing up my sleep. You'd think I'd be past all that by now, but he bothers me terribly, making me, making me . . ."

She twisted so wildly on her chair that she nearly fell off of it.

"Making you want him?" Ruby asked.

She said it calmly and the semi-sister jumped.

"He said you'd understand! He said you'd understand, but I did not believe him!"

Ruby felt a tiny blast of very cold air, and asked quite carefully, "Does the man we are talking about share your desire, and, if so, have you acted on it? Is this a two-way street you are walking down, or are you on it by yourself?"

"Oh, it's a two-way street, all right, but no, we haven't acted on it. . . ."

"One more question, then. I never ask such things, but this time I must. What is your almost lover's name?"

"It's Henry Hyde," said Mary Andrew Michaelsonsen. "It was he who suggested that I call for an appointment."

She paused then added, "'*Our hearts beat together senselessly, sending the clearest message to our loins.*' Tell me now, have you ever heard such beautiful words?"

The unfortunate reply was yes, Ruby had heard such words, whether beautiful or not. And when she heard them again now a sadness shone in though her office window, as if day had turned to night and the moon were painting the two of them with its dull silver brush.

When she stood up, the semi-sister did, too, and promptly left Ruby's office.

"Here's what I think you should do," Ruby called after her. "Go cook up more steaks, and tell *Henry Hyde* that we spoke!"

When she looked at the file again and saw that Mary Andrew lived at the Sisters of Eternal Pity, over on Ninth Avenue, it made her doubly angry. "People don't want pity with their soup; they want to be left alone!" she told her office walls.

Chapter Five

12

RUBY NEARLY HAD TO FORCE the blood out of Gerard's uncooperative arm, but now it sat in tubes, the tubes in an insulated box on her porch, waiting for the lab man to pick them up. A day had passed since the horrible visit from the semi-sister, and Mr. Utterson was coming at six to take her to the soup kitchen, her earlier resolve *not* to go there be damned.

Our hearts beat together senselessly, sending the clearest message to our loins!

If that was nonsense now, how had it not been nonsense when Bob first said it to her last year? And another good question was this: First a dog and then the bunches of flowers? How had things changed from Mr. Utterson's fulfilling his duties to a client to this sense Ruby had that he was courting her? She didn't know, but the sense was so strong that she spent an hour trying to look him up online. She couldn't find a single reference to this Gabriel Utterson, but there were many concerning Henry Jekyll's London friend and lawyer, back in 1886. *That* Mr. Utterson first observed Edward Hyde's dim doorway by gaslight, when out for an evening stroll with Mr. Enfield, and now the lights along

Bank Street made Ruby imagine a similar darkness beyond them, and a presence in that darkness like none she had experienced in her life.

13

It was an ordinary area, not the least bit down-and-out. Businesses and warehouses stood near delis and dry cleaners, by-the-slice pizza shops and Chinese takeout.

Gerard parked his taxi in the block between the Sisters of Eternal Pity soup kitchen and the Boys of Summer halfway house, where he'd lived before moving into Ruby's basement. Boys of Summer had six letters missing from its sign, making it look like B . . . ummer. At its entrance stood a doorman wearing raggedy clothes and a single white glove.

The soup kitchen's entrance was on a side street, where a few people had already lined up. Ruby bought a hijab from a nearby street vendor, and also wore sunglasses, though it was dark. Mary Andrew Michaelsonsen hadn't seen Mr. Utterson when she came to the clinic, so he went as himself, whoever that might be, perhaps as a figment of Bob's imagination, perhaps as a bumbling older man, afraid to take the arm of the disguised woman by his side.

The moment they stepped through the doorway, they saw the semi-sister walking among the tables under bright fluorescent lights, a far more ragged look to her than the one she'd presented in Ruby's office. Her white shirt now seemed gray, her gray skirt wrinkled, her pretty blue Keds wornout at the toes. It seemed that thirty years had passed since Ruby last saw her, not a mere thirty hours.

Mr. Utterson stood in the food line while Ruby huddled behind him, trying to make her pregnancy look like fat.

"It's Swiss steak night," said the woman manning the trays. "Swiss steak doesn't refer to Switzerland, but to a process called swissing. I find that interesting, don't you?"

This woman was white-haired and gap-toothed, wearing yellow horn-rimmed glasses, with her facial features all pointing up. When Mr. Utterson said he did find it interesting, that he had always thought it stood for Switzerland, her mouth climbed even higher into its points, making her look like a triptych of the Swiss Alps.

"Say, do you happen to know if Henry Hyde is here tonight?" Mr. Utterson asked. "If so, we'd like a word with him."

Ruby nearly shoved him into the mashed potatoes, but the horn-rimmed sister put a hand to her brow. "I don't think he's here yet, but you should ask that pretty lady over there!" she said. "Yoo hoo, Mary Andrew! These people are looking for your Mr. Hyde!"

When Mary Andrew turned toward them, Ruby turned, too, and ran back out through the door they'd entered. What had she been thinking, coming here like this? She was this woman's doctor, not Alice down a rabbit hole in someone's else's story!

She hurried toward Mr. Utterson's car, raindrops dotting her sunglasses. Gerard was still in the driver's seat, but when she shook the door handle, he didn't respond, and when she put her eyes against the glass and pounded on it, she saw his hands in his lap, one of them forming the letter *C* again.

"Good Christ, not now!" she shouted.

When the B . . . ummer doorman heard her, then saw her

coming toward him, he used his gloved hand to salute her, and his bare hand to open the door, with no curiosity at all in his expression, even when she ran into his building.

In the hallway, she calmed a little and tried to catch her breath. A tattered orange runner streamed down the center of the floor, with rooms on either side of it, each with a name printed neatly on a rectangle of dirty white paper: *Ms. Bowen, Mr. Washington, Mr. Poole, Mr. Lamb, Mrs. Florentino . . .* She thought there'd be an exit at the hallway's end but found only a stairway going up. Still, she might have climbed it, heading even further into her misery and her mistakes, had a door not opened halfway down the hall behind her and a man come out, turning toward the building's front. She hadn't read the name cards on that side of the hallway but felt she knew what his would say, for he was Henry Jekyll in his gait and posture, Edward Hyde in his bony wrists and hands and curving yellow fingernails. When he passed the doorman, those hands pushed hard against the poor man's chest, even while his lips said cheerfully, "Good evening, Mr. Poole. How's the world treating you? Better than it's treating me, I hope."

Ruby ran back to the door he'd come out of, convinced that she would find some fake name scrawled there, but his card was like his body, with *Henry* in a pretty script, while **HYDE** stood up in caps that dripped like blood off branches.

Henry and **HYDE***!* Though she would question it later, then she was sure that she was seeing it with her own two eyes.

By the time she ran out of the building after him, he was peering into Mr. Utterson's taxi a half a block down. Did he remember riding in it as Archie B. Billingsly? Did he remember his life with her as Bob?

"You!" she nearly shouted, but what would she have said to whatever version of him turned around?

As he loped off toward the soup kitchen, he put up an umbrella, though he hadn't had one before. Had he lifted it from the vendor that Ruby now passed, his *Hyde* hands stealing it while his *Henry* mouth smiled out a happy "Good evening"?

Ruby stopped at Mr. Utterson's car again, to find Gerard as he had been. And she stopped again on the corner across from the soup kitchen to watch *Henry Hyde* line up behind some others, polite and normal, with his hands behind his back.

This was so fantastical! How far did *Hyde* go under cover of *Henry's* clothing? Could a monster who inhabited one's mind also inhabit one's body?

Without question she had seen his lope, but did the blood that flowed through his twisting veins and arteries look like the blood she had taken from Gerard, or was it a roaring, churning sea of sickness and heartache, bent upon the destruction of everyone else?

Chapter Six

14

"HEY, GERARD, WHAT'S UP? Are you okay?"

Ruby'd formed the habit of checking on him several times daily since the horrible night of the soup kitchen—it had taken another hour to wake him up then—and now she worried that he'd fallen into catatonia again.

"Geraldo? Gerrymander?"

She put her face next to his and touched his cheek.

"Look, Dr. Okada!" he shouted. "It says right here, 'Dear, Gerard'!"

He startled her so badly that she fell back against the wall, nearly going into labor. But then, for the first time in a long time, she felt the sweet sense of happiness for someone else. Gerard had an answer from Hal Holbrook!

He read Hal's e-mail to her in his telephone answering machine voice.

"'Dear Gerard, Thanks for your kind note. I must say that though I've run into other Holbrooks, this is the first time one of them has written to me. Thanks, too, for mentioning your poster. It's nice to know that mama pigs let puppies suck their teats.

"'Now, as to whether or not you should go to London and

whether life has its surprises . . . The reason I've taken my time getting back to you is that I've been giving those questions a lot of thought. . . .'"

"He gave them thought because they're good questions," said Ruby.

"Shhh, Dr. Okada, Hal's not finished! And it wasn't just 'thought'; it was 'a lot' of it!"

"'Let's take the second question first,'" he read. "'Of course life has its surprises. From one way of looking at it, that's all life is. I'm surprised to be me, and I'll bet you're surprised to be you. Sam Clemens was surprised to be Mark Twain, by the way. . . . I have that on good authority.

"'Should you go to London now? That's a harder question. It depends on whether you like the idea of prompting life's surprises, or if you believe, as I do, in serendipity. By that I mean, if I were you, I'd stay in New York, stay and see what happens to you. It's only my opinion, of course, so please let me know what you decide to do. It was a pleasure hearing from you, Gerard. Your fellow Holbrookian, Hal.'"

Gerard floated up to the ceiling of the room.

"It's a great reply!" said Ruby. "And now you understand why he took so long."

"And he wants to know what I decide! But Mr. Utterson told me he might not go to London now, that he wants to see how things go here first. Maybe he believes in the Serene Deputy, too, Dr. Okada, just like me and Hal."

"Serene Deputy?" Ruby said a half a second before she fell in love with it.

15

"WELL, SHE WASN'T HAPPY that I've skipped so many appointments, if that's what you mean, but she said the baby's fine. I saw his fingers and toes. . . . And his penis, Bette, my God, it comes down to his knees almost."

Whenever Ruby spoke to Bette, she found herself wanting to sound like her, and also acting a little bawdily. It was one of the reasons she'd decided to stop their friendship. But finally she had called Bette and invited her over for drinks, along with Mr. Utterson. She couldn't do this alone anymore. She needed the opinions that both her oldest and her newest New York friend would have.

Bette got there early and was now in Ruby's kitchen with her, standing at the open backdoor in a white T-shirt with the sparkling blue letters *OMG AKA WTF* stretched across her breasts. Ruby had just told her about Henry Hyde.

"I'll support you, too," said Bette, "I'll always support you. But what if something bad happens? This is nothing to fool around with, Rubes. You remember that much from your doctor years."

The 'too' referred to Ruby's waxing on about the great support she got from Mr. Utterson, the reference to Ruby's 'doctor years' Bette's usual facetiousness.

Bette sat down across from her, her hands around a glass of cold sauvignon blanc.

"I'm not kidding. A lot of bad things happen in those books of his, right? So what are we going to do if he starts acting them out? Henry and Hyde! For fuck sake, Ruby, he's putting the doctor and the monster back together again."

She laughed and sipped her wine, then said, "If we could do that, we'd win the Nobel Prize."

"Never mind that for a second, Bette. What I want to know right now is whether or not you have ever seen dissociative disorder alter someone physically? And I mean *seen it* with your own eyes."

"Well, there was Mr. Mueller, the jeweler, who was diabetic in his normal state but as healthy as a vegan when he was Manny Garcia, the mariachi guitarist," Bette said. "His diabetes disappeared the moment he started ai ya ya ya-ing. . . . But if you promise not to get judgmental on me, let me tell you about someone else."

She paused until Ruby promised. Apparently, she'd been judgmental in the past.

"Do you know what a pillion is?" Bette asked.

Bette was known in the profession as an outlier, as someone quick to source books like *The Golden Bough* or men like Joseph Campbell when dealing with dissociative disorder. She'd once published a paper entitled: "The Ineffable Descent of Ancient Gods, Come to Bother the Modern Mind," nearly ruining her career. It was why she suspected Ruby's question, and it was also why Ruby needed her.

"No," said Ruby, "I don't know what a pillion is."

"It's that place behind the saddle on a horse or a motorcycle where someone else can ride, and I often think of a patient's physical changes like that. I mean, couldn't someone's second personality sit behind the first *as if* on a pillion, perhaps changed physically only because of necessarily hunched shoulders, or from being blown by an the incredible side wind? You'd be changed physically, too, would you not, if you were holding on for dear life?"

She fluttered her eyelids and puffed her T-shirt out.

"Listen to me now," she said, "because I'm not saying this twice. I once lived in Marin County, out in California, on the other side of the Golden Gate Bridge. I was treating a man named Giorgio Paramour, who was twenty-nine years old and drove one of those Italian motorcycles . . . a Ducati . . . The Ducati's what gave me this pillion idea. Giorgio was my final patient every Friday, so we'd often leave my building together, and occasionally he would roar around me on that motorcycle as I made my way back home across the bridge. He wasn't making progress. Drugs were useless, of course, and so, it seemed, was talk therapy. But here's the thing . . . Giorgio ran a men's store out in Sausalito under his real name, which was Gary Johnson. So he had a sort of 'on and off' switch for his disease, which I kept on failing to find."

"Wow," said Ruby. "I wish we could find that switch on Archie. . . ."

"Yes, well, we'll get to that, but one Friday night when we left my office, Giorgio told me he was stopping treatment. He thanked me, forced an envelope into my hands, got on his motorcycle, and roared away. I tried to stop him, but it happened so fast! I just stood there listening to that high-pitched Ducati. The envelope contained an extra five hundred bucks, plus two tickets to the San Francisco Opera company's production of *La Traviata* for that very night."

"Generous," said Ruby. "Dissociative disorder patients are usually as poor as church mice."

"Poorer than," Bette said, "and I was deeply upset by his quitting. But the opera was the opera, and *La Traviata* was right up my alley, so I took the tickets home, and ended up going with Tom, my husband at the time. I kept scanning the audience for Giorgio; during intermission, I even worked my way backstage, sure that he would be there, in charge of costume design. . . .

"Oh, I haven't told this right. He took his 'Giorgio Paramour' handle from a nineteenth-century costume designer at Milan's famous opera house, La Scala. I discovered it during my initial research, when I thought he was malingering.

"Anyway, he wasn't backstage, so when the opera ended, I was the first one outside, searching for him among the departing fans. Tom noticed my behavior and thought I was on the lookout for an entirely different kind of paramour, but I couldn't leave it alone. The next morning, I went to Sausalito and discovered at the men's store that Gary Johnson had ridden his Ducati off the Golden Gate Bridge the night before, not twenty minutes after giving up on therapy."

"Oh, Bette, my God, I'm sorry," said Ruby. "Why have you never told me this before?"

"Well, aside from the obvious reason, because it broke my heart. I canceled my appointments, and do you know where I found myself two days later?"

Ruby said without pausing, "Milan."

"Bingo! They have this fabulous costume museum two doors down from La Scala. Now here comes the obvious reason that I haven't told you or anyone else. . . . It took no time at all for me to find a photo of *my* Giorgio Paramour standing in front of La Scala one hundred fucking years ago, Ruby, himself beside a poster of the opera that was playing that night, which, wouldn't you know it, was *La Traviata*."

"Maybe Gary Johnson saw that poster, too, and made himself up to look like Giorgio. Malingerers can be terrific schemers."

"I know they can, but he had a mole so prominently displayed on his chin that I asked him once if he'd seen an oncologist, and that mole was in the La Scala picture, too. To make sure he hadn't manufactured the mole to look like the old-time Giorgio's, I called and asked Tom to go to Gary's funeral and check it out. They'd fished him out of the bay right after I left for Milan."

"And they buried the mole with Gary Johnson?"

"Food for thought, don't you think? It is my belief that there are true metaphysical rovers in the world, Ruby, but if you put that in an academic paper these days, they throw you under the bus."

She looked at Ruby as if to say, Even your friends do sometimes, but Ruby only asked, "Who was driving and who sat on the pillion when he drove off the Golden Gate Bridge?"

"Giorgio was driving, of course," said Bette. "Long before that night, the Gary in Gary could only ride along, *except* when he ran his menswear store. For eight hours a day, he was Gary, maybe only because he had to make a living, but something made him normal for that period of time."

When she stood and pulled the wine bottle from the fridge, Ruby saw that insulin box and got up to go find Guido.

She'd forgotten to give him his shot again.

16

WHEN MR. UTTERSON ARRIVED a half hour later, he opened the bottle of the Lagavulin he'd brought, pouring himself a drink.

"Where's Gerard?" he asked. "I need to set a few things straight with him."

"He's downstairs, waiting for Godot," said Ruby.

She paused, then added, "In this case, Godot is Hal Holbrook."

Mr. Utterson sipped his whiskey. He looked disheveled, maybe a little bit drunk.

"I hate to say it, but in this case, Godot is me," he said finally. "When I couldn't find Hal Holbrook's e-mail address, I made one up, and used it to write to Gerard. He won't understand why I did it, but I feel I've got to tell him anyway. Oh, who but a fool could do a thing like that—introduce guile into the heart of such a guileless man?"

He frowned when Bette came into the parlor, then pretended to be frowning at the scotch. He'd thought that he and Ruby were alone.

"Don't mind me," said Bette. "As far as I'm concerned, there's nothing wrong with a fake Hal Holbrook e-mail. Probably even better than the real thing."

"And saying Gerard won't understand isn't the half of it," Ruby added. "If you tell him what you've done, he'll break like Humpty Dumpty, Gabriel, and we won't be able to put him back together again."

It was the first time she had ever called him Gabriel, though she'd been thinking of Humpty Dumpty a lot.

She looked from him to Bette, introduced the two of them, then sat beside him on the couch, beneath her father's de Kooning knockoff and in front of his emerald green coffee table. Her father could make something fake and it would be beautiful, for in his way he was as guileless as Gerard.

"Surely you don't think I should write him again?" Mr. Utterson asked, but when Bette sat down on his other side, for the moment he shut up about Gerard. Neither of her guests had seen them earlier, but Ruby had all three Archie Billingsly photos with her—Archie S., Archie O., and Archie B.—plus the oldest version of Anna Stevenson Billingsly. She set them on the coffee table, poured some scotch for Bette, and a half ounce of it for herself.

"What we have here are Archie's grandfather, his father, and Archie himself, all in their early to mid-twenties, and all looking healthy. So here's the deal. . . . I asked you here so we could get to the bottom of whatever's going on, and I think that the bottom of it is staring us right in the face."

Bette picked up the photo of "Archie himself."

"I don't know about healthy, since this is how he looked when he arrived at the hospital and told me that voices were coming out of his mouth," she said. "Not much question that he was fucked-up then."

"The voices came out of his mouth?" Mr. Utterson asked. "I thought schizophrenics heard their voices in their heads. Maybe he's just a ventriloquist."

When neither woman laughed, he poured himself more scotch. There was a "lonely rooster" look to him now, prompted by the way his hair stood up on his head.

"Yes, well, I thought schizophrenia, too, for a couple of minutes, but he said it so calmly, like another might mention the weather or that he should have worn a coat," said Bette. "Still, I fiddled around with various schizophrenia schematics, none of which worked. Half the time I suspected malingering . . . just a guy who felt like seeing if he could fool the experts, like a Daniel Day-Lewis or a Meryl fucking Streep. . . . But the other half of the time I was convinced that his was the rarest condition I had ever come across."

She nodded at Ruby, as if saying, Just about as rare as Giorgio's.

"Once he was a sea captain, terrifically knowledgeable regarding tides and sea-lanes and such, but he was never Jekyll or Hyde, nor the amalgam of them that you two apparently ran across at the soup kitchen. I would have told you this at dinner if you'd shown up at Bon Bonito that night, Ruby, but what I wanted us to write about *inside* Archie's illness was his superior knowledge, and where that knowledge might have come from. Dissociatives are often full of feelings, but without much learning and without the wherewithal to get it. When he became that sea captain, though, he knew every bit of what sea captains know, and could express it with depth and clarity. That's why I didn't buy into dissociative disorder at all."

While Bette talked, Ruby rested her hands on her belly, her baby kicking slightly beneath them. She had her own agenda for the evening, and this wasn't it.

"Hold that thought," she said. "There's something else I want to ask before I forget. What was Archie wearing when you admitted him to the hospital? I mean that very first day."

Bette took the whiskey from Mr. Utterson, clearly irritated with the change of subject. "How the fuck do I know what he was wearing?" she said. "Maybe chinos and a shirt?"

"Chinos and a shirt, yet he was decked out in a Scottish tweed jacket when I met him by the elevator. So he had to have had Bob's clothing stashed somewhere, and that means he had knowledge of Bob when he wasn't Bob, right?"

"All I know is that he was a knowledgeable sea captain," Bette muttered, but Mr. Utterson said, "Oh ho, Ruby, you're right! One can make up voices, even a good bit of sea knowledge, but one cannot make up a Harris tweed coat!"

"It's true that for the fourteen days of his initial visit he didn't leave the hospital, and he had no visitors," Bette said.

"On the other hand, maybe Bob's clothing was in his roller bag when he got to the hospital. Maybe Bob packed the bag, left it for Archie to take, then opened it and put the clothes on when he was Bob again!"

Mr. Utterson stood up and started to pace, excited to be making such progress. "He's just like Hal Holbrook in his Mark Twain suit," he said. "He doesn't become Mark Twain until he's ready to go onstage."

"But Hal Holbrook's acting. He knows he's acting and the audience knows it and there's a time limit. Ninety minutes later, he's back to being Hal," said Bette.

She stuck out her chest, both barrels aimed at Mr. Utterson.

"If we take it one step further, though," she said, "and say that an actor who doesn't know he's acting has dissociative disorder . . . well, then the question still is, Where does his knowledge come from?"

As she always did, Bette brought things back to where she wanted them. And when Mr. Utterson helped her by saying, "It has to come from study, and the studier had to be Archie," Ruby pulled the Anna Stevenson Billingsly photo onto her lap, wiping its glass on her shirt. She was going to say "It doesn't take a genius to suspect that she might be the master link," but with one sharp kick from her coming child, all of her energy went out of her.

So she sat there watching them talk.

Chapter Seven

17

GERARD'S BLOOD TESTS CAME BACK, Ruby ran them again, and they came back once more. His cholesterol was 432, his A1C numbers were consistent with diabetes, and he had a body-mass index of 40.7.

She wrote prescriptions and made him a chart as big as his pig poster, outlining when he should take which pills. In this way, she shifted her thoughts from the complex diagnosis of the father of her child to the worrisome condition of a mosaic man she had grown to love. This went on for nearly three weeks, until the second Monday of October, when Gerard stood waiting for her in front of her clinic as she came back from her lunchtime walk.

"Guess what, Dr. Okada," he said. "Someone just went into our backyard."

He pulled a notepad from his pocket and read what he'd written on it in his telephone voice. "At 1:04 on October eighth, 2012, a man with a bleeding leg went through our back gate."

"Wait!" said Ruby. "*What?* You mean he's in there now?"

She didn't have to be told who the man was.

"Unless he went into the house," Gerard said.

The only other ways out of the backyard were up the stairs into the kitchen or down the stairs into her clinic, and both those doors were locked.

"Tell me now, Gerard, and no fooling around. How do you know his leg was bleeding? Could you see it? Did he tell you? And what did this man look like?"

"First he walked slowly and then he walked fast," Gerard said. "And I know his leg was bleeding, because there was blood on his pants."

Ruby's initial thought was to call Bette or Mr. Utterson, but when Gerard turned and walked through the side gate, slowly and then fast, to show her how the man had walked, what could she do but follow him. Still, she texted both her friends, saying "Come quickly!" before putting her phone in her pocket.

The clouds were dark and pushed together, threatening rain. She didn't want to get too far behind Gerard, coming upon him only after the man had asked for some damned thing like cheese and then disappeared again. So as soon as she caught him, she took his arm.

"We're in this together," she said. "No one goes off on their own, okay, Gerard?"

"Like the lion and Dorothy in *The Wizard of Oz*," Gerard said. "Only I'm not cowardly, Dr. Okada."

"You definitely aren't cowardly, but I am, so let me stick with you. And what do you think? Should I call to him? If there's any of Bob left in him, I think he'll know my voice. . . . And Archie will probably know it, too."

Before Gerard could answer, she said, "Hello out there? I'd like to have a word with you."

The moment she spoke, and without any evidence at all, she knew that he was Archie, standing just out of sight.

"Hi there, Archie," she said. "We've never been properly introduced, and I have never properly thanked you for the house."

"Hello," said a voice, unmistakably Bob's.

She stepped in front of Gerard, a hand held up behind her.

"Bob, is it you?" she asked. "Do you remember being Archie? Do you know who you've been after you've been him, or who you're going to be before you are?"

But those were entirely the wrong questions. For the moment, she should simply have asked him to let her take a look at his leg.

"Nothing is clear to me," he said. "I have tried to make them so, but just as with dreams, clarity floats away upon awakening."

His voice came from beyond a wall of trees. She said, "Your child is here, too. Would you like to come touch him?"

She knew that he would show himself, but he did not. It was as if he were locked inside a safe, waiting for the right combination of words.

"What if I give you a really good look at him?" she asked.

Though she was still aware of Gerard behind her, she unbuttoned her shirt, and when she pulled it apart, her bulging belly came out.

"Come put your hands on him," she said. "That's a father's right, and I bet he'll know your touch."

She stared at a break in the foliage ahead of her, but he stepped out six feet to her left. He wore a collarless shirt, with suspenders looping his shoulders, his hair was parted in the middle, and his right trouser leg was bloodied from the top of his thigh to his knee.

"What Makes a Loved One?" was a poem he'd written for her once, and when she asked him to recite it, he did.

> *Oh, what makes a loved one?*
> *Is it chemical or mineral,*
> *Brought upon waves that*
> *Strike the lighthouse*
> *Eleven miles out?*
>
> *Oh, what makes one love?*
> *What made Juliet glance*
> *Across the room at*
> *Just that moment?*
> *Was it, perchance, a sound?*

She couldn't help thinking that it wasn't a very good poem.

"Can't you simply stay with me, Bob?" she asked when he was done. "Or stay with me *as* Bob, I guess I mean to say."

"For a time I thought I could, but I cannot."

She felt the sting of that but hid it behind an enigmatic smile.

"Well, don't be afraid to touch our son at least. You, with your brilliance, formed him, along with me and my incompetence."

She used a needy voice, a voice that no one ought to want to hear, but it worked well enough to make him fall to his knees and put his hands up, his fingers bent toward her, still, absolutely, the man she had loved. When he shuffled across the dirt that way, she steeled herself against her desire to turn and run by waiting for the touch of those fingers with her eyes closed. And even when she felt them, she stayed that way— until she also felt him stand and heard his voice grow crisp, coming out of his mouth in a conspiratorial way. She knew from just the sound of it that Bob was gone.

"We know you're needed aboard the Hispaniola, *but could you take a proper look at her?"* said the voice. *"It would be good if we could put this pregnancy thing to rest."*

Though it wasn't exactly Archie speaking, when she opened her eyes, she first saw Archie's face. And then she saw it change in part to someone else's, and heard similar words to those she'd known from reading *Treasure Island* in her childhood tree house.

"I will, if I must, but please be quick about it, for urgent matters await me on the *Hispaniola*," said Dr. David Livesey, "and to miss my next lines would be catastrophic. A novel's no good if its characters start to leave it, going off for various medical consultations." He looked on the ground around him, as if in search of a hat. "But of course I'll take a look at her, and pardon my impatience," he said. "On shipboard it's nothing but cutlass wounds and scurvy. I'm glad to help, for a troublesome pregnancy make the worries of pirates seem crass. I wrote my medical thesis on melancholia, you know. Perhaps that's why you called me."

"There's nothing troublesome about my pregnancy," said Ruby. "In fact, I got a good report on it just the other week. It's pinning down the father that is causing me fits."

But Dr. Livesey ignored her, only putting on his invisible hat.

"After months at sea a phenomenon assails me when I reach solid land," he said. "It feels like the whole world pitches sideways, making me think that any kind of steadiness is an illusion. I know, of course, that it's only my inner ear, but that is the feeling of it, nevertheless. Now, let's get to it. Tell me your name."

"I am Ruby Gail Okada, as if you didn't know."

"Well then, Ruby Gail, there's a doctor's here to see you, come from the world's wide oceans," he said. "He goes by the name of Livesey. Would you give him a moment of your time?"

He seemed to find the self-introduction charming.

"A lively man, you say?" she asked.

"I do often hope that I'm a lively man, but Livesey is my name. I'm a melancholy expert with scurvy background. Now, tell me what the trouble is. Are you ill, or faking it, or is this a case of love gone wrong? The father gone off when the going gets tough."

"*Ill* might be the word for it," she said, "for I'm carrying a sick man's child. But I'm going to raise it healthily and well."

"How do you know the man was sick? Maybe he's just tricky. Sometimes a thing can look one way yet be another."

His voice grew soft and his eyes grew moist. He held both of his slender hands out in front of her, then put one up in a way that blocked her view of his eyes. And then he whispered, as if to someone else, *"Sounds like a perspective problem to me. She thinks she's pregnant, but what she thinks is wrong. As long as her mind believes it, however, her body will continue to agree. You have to disabuse her of that notion."*

"Whom are you talking to, and how can you say such a thing?" Ruby asked. "I'm as big as a globe of the world, with all of its continents kicking at me."

He dropped his hand again, so she could once more see his eyes. He also dropped his whisper. "Is there some idea within you that you might not want to keep your baby?" he asked. "That you might pass the difficulties of raising it on to someone else?"

"No idea of that at all. I'm his mother and will be his mother through stormy seas and calm ones. And if things go on as they're going on now, I'll keep his father's identity from him until he turns eighteen and can decide whether he wants to know about him or not. Though I myself am beginning to think that his father's a bit of a lout."

"I can see that you're determined, but consider your anger at the father. Will it not turn you into a 'spare the rod and spoil the child' kind of parent?"

He hid his eyes again. *"Note her next answer,"* he whispered, *"for it will tell us the truth about her pregnancy."*

"I'll never spoil the child and spare the rod," said Ruby.

"Aha! Just as I suspected, you said it topsy-turvy," Dr. Livesey said. "It's a classic example of Compton's word reversal syndrome, and it means that your pregnancy is false!"

His voice had such a sense of triumph to it that it was nearly impossible for Ruby to remember that he wasn't a real doctor, that all these characters were being played by the same man.

"Really? Compton's word reversal syndrome?" she said. "In all my years of study, I never heard of that one."

"Yes, brilliant man, Compton. I met him once in London. But I have lines to say on Treasure Island, so I'd better go say them. My opinion is that you're not pregnant, and that your family and friends ought not mollycoddle this ghost pregnancy. Making light of Compton's word reversal syndrome is a secondary symptom of the syndrome itself, by the way. If left untreated, it can lead to nervous breakdown."

"You say you have lines to say on Treasure Island, but do you even remember what your next lines are?"

"Of course I remember them," Dr. Livesey said.

He then closed his eyes and pulled the lines from somewhere deep inside of him. *"The tide keeps washing her down. Could you pull a little stronger? We'll never get ashore at this rate."*

Ruby wanted to tell him that she hadn't been making light of Compton's word reversal syndrome, but by then it was too late.

18

THE HOUSE HAD A THIRD-FLOOR ROOM with a window in its door and an actual doorbell in its frame. During Archie's childhood—during all three Archies' childhoods, probably—it had been a playroom, for it still held toys and smallish furniture—a bed, a writing desk, and the cars and locomotives of an old electric train.

He turned back into Archie when she said she'd like to take him inside. He even seemed appreciative, a Ulysses of the dissociative set, finally getting home after years and years of trying. He let Ruby remove his pants before she put him on the bed, his knife wound opening and closing each time he flexed his thigh. When she threw his pants on a nearby chair, one leg crossed the other, making it seem as if the lower half of someone's body were engaged in casual socializing.

"I'm going to sew this cut up now, give it a chance to heal," Ruby said. "No worries even if it hurts a bit; it's not the kind of pain that sticks around, okay?"

She showed him her suture kit. "Tell me it's all right if I do this now, and clean and dress your wound, and find you something clean to wear."

"Dress my wound if you must, but I would rather have you *redress* my complaints against my family," he said.

He nodded in a way that let her know he remembered the room, and then toward an open bathroom door. "And a bath would certainly warm me," he said. "I'm as cold as a warm-blooded man could possibly be."

Gerard stood behind them, just as he had outside.

"I'm good at running baths," he said. "I like a three bears bath myself, not too hot and not too cold, but just right!"

When he went to draw the bath, Ruby cleaned and sutured Archie's wound, helped him stand, then walked him toward the bathroom, the door to which swung back and forth like a door might swing in the wind of an abandoned house. It might have been a sign of danger brewing, but she had set her course. When she got him on the toilet seat and started to take off the rest of his clothes, however, he reached out to touch her abdomen again. And then, once more, he was Bob.

"My son, do you know me? I lived in a house with a big red door. Did you not live there, too, in the mossy green inkling of my foreknowledge?"

Ruby brought a hand up from her side in order to touch his cheek. That he was Bob again did not surprise her, for Bob, like any man would, wanted contact with his child. But she said, "Let's speak a little more plainly. And a good place to start is with you telling me your name."

"I was Rob to my mother, Son to my father when his anger subsided, and Robbie to Cummy, my nursemaid. I was frailty itself to my doctors, but in my world of make-believe I was whoever I chose to be—a highlands bagpiper, a fisherman who lost his brother in a storm. . . ."

"When Bette was your doctor, you weren't any of those

things. When Bette was your doctor, you were Archie B. Bill-ingsly, most of the time, at least, third in a line of deeply trou-bled Archies, each with a different middle name."

It hadn't surprised Ruby to see Bob come back again, but it surprised her a little now to see him grow startled on the toilet seat.

"There's an Archie in my novel, *Weir of Hermiston,*" he said, "though people often refer to him as *Erchie*. His life would have been most like my own, had I been given the time to finish the book."

"An unfinished Archie in an unfinished novel?" Ruby asked. "We have three Archies here whose lives couldn't find a proper course. I am trying to save the third of them now. I don't think we need a fourth."

But Bob was caught up in his book.

"Listen to this," he said. *"'Mind, Maister Erchie dear, that this life's a' disappointment, and a mouthfu' o' mools is the appointed end.' Mools* means 'mounds' and mounds means earth, and the whole thing means that when we die, mounds of earth are what we're filled with."

"Did *you* ever have such fears? Did the Archie in your novel?"

"He had no such fears at the time I stopped work, and since I am here now with no such fears myself, I would like to finish the story, see if the acts of *Erchie's* life bring those fears to bear in him. I saw a little desk a moment ago. . . . Might I ask you to let me go work at it when my bath is done? And would you provide me with writing materials?"

Ruby put a hand over the edge of the tub.

"The water's ready now," she said.

When she tried to help him stand, his penis swung in front

of her like the pendulum of a slowly dying clock. She also saw an unmistakable streak of purple hematoma running down his thigh below her sutures.

"Tell me again how your leg got hurt," she said.

Refracted by the water once he sat in it, both Bob's legs looked misshapen.

She turned the hot water on again, then looked around for soap.

"Gerard, would you go get a bar of soap and one of those big towels from my bathroom?" she called out to the bedroom, where Gerard still waited.

Gerard left quickly, and when he was gone, Ruby sat on the tub's narrow rim, her abdomen now near Bob's face. When he pulled a hand from the water and drew a line across her abdomen, at the spot where a C-section incision might go, she thought he might make the sign of the cross, but his second line was parallel to the first, an equals sign, though nothing equaled anything anymore.

She pushed one of her hands beneath the water to press it atop his wound, and when she brought it up again, a question mark of pus sat on her palm.

"I've got penicillin in my clinic. Maybe Mr. Utterson will get it for us when he comes."

She thought of Mr. Utterson, though she'd texted both him and Bette.

"Do you mean *my* Mr. Utterson?" he asked. "How can a figment of my imagination bring me the medicine to make me well again?"

When she nodded, he nodded, as if both of them thought that was a pretty good point.

Chapter Eight

19

SOME OF IT HIT HER IN THE BATHROOM, to be sure, but as Ruby worked her way downstairs after she and Gerard finally talked Bob out of finishing *Weir of Hermiston* and succeeded in putting Archie to bed, it suddenly seemed that no one before her had ever felt such deep exhaustion.

She meant to get the penicillin and go immediately back upstairs to try to do whatever she could for him. She knew there were time limits to whatever she was into now, but when she stopped in her bedroom and sat on her bed for just a moment's rest, the world disappeared until well after noon the next day, and returned in a rush with Gerard's upset voice.

"I know that! You don't have to tell me that, because I know it!"

"Maybe you know it, but you didn't do it," Bette barked. "What was our rule from the moment we got here? I know you know the rule, because I've already made you say it twice."

"Lock the lock and keep the key in my pocket."

"No! Lock the lock and give the key back to me or Mr. Utterson!"

Ruby stumbled to her feet, sat back down, and stumbled to her feet again.

"How are things with his leg?" she called. "Did anyone give him antibiotics?"

Her voice didn't work well, but Bette appeared in her doorway, arms folded neatly across her chest.

"I gave him half a million units of penicillin twice," she said. "Gerard got it for me from your clinic. . . . He knows where you keep your drugs, Ruby, I don't think that's a very good thing for him to know."

"Half a million units twice? Isn't that too much? And you could be nicer to Gerard, you know. . . . He doesn't respond very well to yelling."

"Ruby, wake up! We weren't here twenty minutes this morning before Long John fucking Silver showed up. What a dangerous thing you've done, bringing him into your house like this! He's sleeping now, but the first time I stuck a needle into him, Gerard and Mr. Utterson had to hold him down. And Gerard responds just fine to yelling. You're the one who never likes to raise her voice."

Ruby still couldn't think straight. When Bette left her alone again, she went into her bathroom, stripped, showered, then stood in front of a full-length mirror. Her abdomen stuck out hugely.

"Ghost pregnancy, my ass," she said.

Soon she'd be a mother, and not long after that her son would stand before a mirror like this one, and not long after that he would leave her just as she had left her father, to deal with ghosts and baggage of his own.

Ain't life fun? she asked herself.

She dried, dressed in a pair of blue stretch jeans and a clean gray sweatshirt, wrapped a towel around her head, and went out to join the fracas.

But when she climbed the stairs to where she thought the fracas would be, no one was there save whoever lay inside that room on the bed. His door had a padlock on it now, but she could see him through its window, wrists tied to the bedstead with some kind of cloth. He'd kicked off his blanket and was staring directly at her, the cords in his neck like ropes, his eyes like the eyes of the devil in films.

"I can't do anything for you now. I don't have the key to this lock," she said.

"'I can't do anything for you!'" he mocked.

The "for you" came like venom from his mouth.

"Okay, then, who are you now?"

"If I am the chief of sinners. I am the chief of sufferers also."

He twisted until his wrists showed chaffing and a smattering of blood.

"Hello, Mr. Hyde," Ruby said.

"How do you know I'm Hyde? Is there something displeasing, something downright detestable about my appearance?"

"How's your thigh? Does it burn or itch? Someone better take another look at it soon. I'm worried that it might be infected."

"Who can worry about a cut when the body surrounding it rages? If you drain a swamp of its rancid water, do you think it's like draining a pond?"

He looked at the floor, as if he might find a swamp there, while she kept looking straight at him, and thinking of Daniel Day-Lewis.

"Do you happen to remember Mary Andrew Michaelsonsen?" Ruby asked. "I don't know why, exactly, but I've got a feeling that she's the one who cut your leg."

"Mary Andrew the half nun from hell! She's a no-good

do-gooder and a simpering doormat! She turns forgiveness into an art!"

So the Hyde in him remembered and hated what the Jekyll in him knew and loved.

"No telling for anyone's taste," she said, "she loved the man she loved."

"*You* say she loved him, I say she showed no respect! If you saw a door marked 'Do Not Enter!' would you not pause before flinging it open? She's Mary Andrew Butinski, that's who she is!"

The chaffing around his wrists was pink.

"You didn't harm her, did you?" asked Ruby. "Where is Mary Andrew now?"

"She's in a world of hurt and a muddle of her own making! But I'm not singing any more of that particular song until you pay the piper. Come tuck my blanket around me, and bring me some water. And touch my penis like you did last night."

"You know as well as I do that I didn't touch your penis, and didn't I just tell you that I don't have the key? . . . But I do have some photos of you when you were young . . . you and the Archies before you. I'll bring them, if you like, and I'll bring Mr. Utterson, too, since you claimed that he was *your* Mr. Utterson last night."

She didn't think he would speak again, but he offered a riddle.

"Do you know what Utterson uttered when he tried to sniff me out before? If you can answer that, I'll look at your pictures. *If* you don't forget my water."

"I do know what Utterson uttered. It was 'If he be Mr. Hyde, I shall be Mr. Seek.'"

"Drats!" he said. "There's no one more despicable than an eavesdropper!"

20

"He wrote me again," said Gerard. "He said he's going on tour soon and doesn't like to e-mail when he's traveling."

"It was good of him to tell you. E-mail etiquette is strange, Gerard. I read online that it's okay to ignore them."

Ruby was struck by Mr. Utterson's decision to end his Hal Holbrook charade this way, without telling Gerard the truth, but also without continuing it. She was struck by the words *on tour,* too. Could she say that Archie was "on tour" with his legions of other personalities?

She had come downstairs expecting to have to defend herself for taking him in, but Mr. Utterson and Bette were in her clinic by then, sitting with the very woman she had just asked Mr. Hyde about; Mary Andrew Michaelsonsen.

Gerard had waited for Ruby upstairs, so he could tell her his latest Hal Holbrook news, and he followed her downstairs now.

"Its hard to e-mail when you travel," he said. "But he'll probably send me another one when he gets home."

"Do you remember me?" Mary Andrew Michaelsonsen asked.

Though, of course, she remembered her, Ruby would not have recognized her had she seen her on the street.

"Would you like to come into my office?" she asked.

"I would not," she said. "Anything I have to say, I can say out here."

Was she hiding a knife under her coat, waiting for the chance to stab him again?

"I used to think there was such a thing as human warmth," she said. "I used to believe in charity and kindness toward others. . . ."

Her face cracked open, but then healed itself back up again.

"Would you like a cup of tea?" Gerard asked. "We have black tea and green tea and yellow tea with ginger in it. We also have Nescafé Gold Blend freeze-dried coffee."

His face was as packed with human warmth as a face could be, and brought the smallest spark of it back into their visitor's eyes.

"I used to drink Nescafé Gold Blend during my student days," she said. "I used to take it with milk."

When Gerard asked the others if they wanted any, and they all said yes, he ran back upstairs to get the coffee.

"While we're waiting, may I ask whether he ever put a 'Keep Out' sign on his door?" Ruby said. "Did he ever want time alone, in order to collect himself, perhaps?"

Ruby imagined his various personalities strewn across his floor, a bit like her old pregnancy clothes. She imagined him hurrying to pick them up.

"His sign said, 'Do Not Enter,'" the semi-sister told her.

She wriggled out of her coat, dropping it over the back of her chair.

"But you entered anyway? In my experience, signs usually mean what they say," said Bette.

"I didn't think of it as a warning. I thought of it as a cry for help."

"Right," said Mr. Utterson. "Sometimes 'Do Not Enter' means 'Come on in.'"

"Was there evidence of a change in him before he put the sign on his door?" Ruby asked. "Were there times, for example, when he wasn't Henry Hyde, but someone else?"

"Of course there were. I'm not a fool and I'm not blind. Sometimes he was terribly grouchy. But I felt that to embrace the worst in him would be a test of my love."

"Terribly grouchy . . ." Bette said. "Good diagnosis there."

The tears that came out of Mary Andrew's eyes made tracks down the dirt on her face, but Ruby pressed on.

"What happened after you ignored his sign?" she asked. "What did you find behind that door?"

"I knew he was alone in his room, but it sounded like someone was in there with him, giving him a terrible beating. And when I burst in, I saw bumps rising up all over him, first here, then there, on his neck and face but also on his arms and shoulders. . . . It was like watching the knobby spine of a sea creature, never quite breaking the surface of his skin. After a while I saw Henry leave his body and also leave the room just as clearly as I would have had he opened the window and crawled out. And what was left was something I couldn't bare to look at. . . ."

Despite her tears, she spoke without much passion, the way crime witnesses do after violence departs. She paused, then asked, "What is that thing a butterfly abandons?"

"A butterfly abandons a chrysalis," Mr. Utterson said.

"A chrysalis, yes, but, after all, that's not correct, for a chrysalis is a discarded husk, while what was left after Henry left the room was very much alive. It was like that Charles Darwin thing, natural selection, had boiled him down to the very worst, not only in him but in all of us."

When she pulled her sweatshirt over her head, they saw that

from where her neck fit into her body cavity, deep scratches traveled south and into the top of her bra.

"It doesn't hurt, but could you put something on it, maybe some salve or ointment? I don't want to take on any more infection than I already have."

Bette went into Ruby's office for a basin and a first-aid kit. She came back out and knelt before the wounded woman, put ointment on some cotton balls, and ran them into the deepest furrows first, then into the shallower ones.

"What happened next?" Mr. Utterson asked.

His face was so full of grief by then that Ruby took his hand.

The man who did this to her was upstairs now, perhaps as Archie, perhaps as Jekyll or Hyde, but the same man nevertheless, with the same lean body and far-apart eyes.

"What happened next? He scratched me badly and was about to fall upon me until he sated himself—his sating tool was bared and at the ready—but then he took a knife from his table and stuck it into his leg instead. He told me later that he was aiming for his heart but that he no longer knew where it was."

Ruby knew where *her* heart was; it had come up and was pounding in her throat.

"So you followed him over here?" asked Bette. "Waited outside all night long?"

"Yes, and now I've come inside. Do you think I could see him? I've a feeling that there's no sign on his door right now."

"Whatever is going on with him, it isn't a test of your love," said Ruby. "And what do you mean, he told you later he was aiming for his heart? Did you have another conversation with him after he stabbed himself?"

"Why, yes, I did, for after he cut himself, the good in him came back. That is why I need to talk to him, don't you see? So he'll know that there is one steadfast person in his life."

When Gerard brought their Nescafé Gold Blend coffee, they all sat drinking it quietly.

21

THOSE FAMILIAR WITH THE THEORY of probability would likely calculate that things weren't looking good for Archie B. Billingsly, but whatever his odds, thus began a ten-day period of everyone sleeping at the house, and each, in turn, attempting to be the steadfast person in his life.

Why a ten-day period?

Because at the end of it, Ruby's father arrived . . . and life for Archie and the rest of them began to imitate art.

PART

TWO

Chapter Nine

22

KENJI OKADA GREW UP on the southern Japanese island of Kyushu, where he learned to love breadfruit. He was born in 1944—the same year as Archie O. Billingsly—but at the age of twenty-two moved north and east to Kyoto in order to work with the great American artist Jack Madson, and to hang out at a bar called Jittoku, drinking and carousing with other Japanese artists and with foreigners. His artistic interests were as disparate as the chair and desk he'd made for Ruby were from his eternally dripping teapot, as his de Kooning knockoff (made when he was thinking of forgery) was from his own paintings and drawings. His only failure in whatever he tried, in all of the realms of art, came when he attempted to carve a traditional Japanese Noh mask, for though he imagined a powerful female character from a play he had seen many times, what his knife carved into his block of cypress was a round-faced woman with weirdly bobbed hair and a faraway look in her eyes. Seeing the woman so shocked him that he gave up Noh masks after only that one attempt, using what remained of his cypress to carve little replicas of netsuke instead.

After a decade or so in Kyoto, Kenji packed his tools and

brushes and moved to Tacoma, Washington, not because it was the center of standard American English, as he liked to tell his daughter, but because it had been the hometown of Richard Brautigan, a novelist whose writing initially influenced his art.

He was only in Tacoma for a few short weeks, living in a small apartment near Wright Park, when he saw Gail Radcliffe and followed her. Gail was on her way to work at the Parkway Tavern, which, quite like Jittoku had been in Kyoto, soon became Kenji's haunt. He was afraid of Gail but loved her. He loved her because he believed she was meant to be his wife, and he believed she was meant to be his wife because when he pulled that Noh mask from the bottom of his trunk, he found that it bore Gail's face, complete with her faraway look and oddly bobbed hair. He was afraid of Gail because he knew she wouldn't love him in return.

Kenji wrapped the Noh mask in a *furoshiki* and carried it to the Parkway Tavern many nights in a row before finding the courage to place it on the bar with Gail's name written on a card on its top. The card read Gail *Lad*cliffe instead of *Rad*cliffe, but when she unwrapped the *furoshiki* and saw the mask, she loved him anyway. Gail had, in fact, loved Kenji since he started coming to the Parkway, but she had had similar fears to his, so she kept her love to herself.

Their only child was born in 1976.

Gail wanted to name her Ruby after her mother, and Kenji wanted to name her Gail after Gail.

That Kenji often called the baby Luby, in a sweet reminiscence of *Lad*cliffe, somehow glued the family together like nothing else could have. He found and repaired an old piano and learned to play the Thelonious Monk tune, "Ruby, My Dear" on it as a bedtime lullaby for his daughter.

But then, five years after Ruby's birth, Gail got sick and died—of congestive heart failure.

During her illness, Ruby promised God that if He would let her mother live, she would become a doctor in order to help spare others (without God's intervention) of similar fates. And though God didn't listen, she became a doctor anyway . . . or at least she became a psychiatrist. And now she was pregnant with a child of her own.

Once her father got to know his grandson, he would learn a different Monk tune and play it on the piano in Ruby's parlor.

He said the tune would likely be "Well, You Needn't," for he thought its title was a good rule upon which build a life.

The bedroom across from Ruby's would be her father's when he arrived.

He'd said he would get there well before his grandson's birth, at the latest by October 20, but trouble with an installation at the Tacoma Art Museum   knockoff Giacometti figures he had made and broken and scattered across the main museum floor—delayed his arrival until October 27, just ahead of Hurricane Sandy. So it was seventeen or eighteen days, not ten, during which the others continued their Archie watch. And they also watched the weather reports for lowland flooding and subway stoppages.

The first thing Ruby's father thought of when he entered the house—to Gerard's and Francesca's greeting in the hallway—was a series of drawings of Down syndrome people, cartoonish but serious, à la that old *Mad* magazine cartoonist Don Martin. And the first thing he said, after putting down his bags, was that he was used to having a madman in the attic, though the attic in question had always been in his head before.

Mr. Utterson and Bette were out, he at his office, she at her hospital—Hurricane Sandy making them batten down the hatches.

"I'm so glad you're here, Dad," said Ruby. "I can't do this without you."

She patted her abdomen, but he knew that wasn't what she meant. She was the psychiatrist in the family, maybe, but he was the shaman, the magician, the spot-on diviner of the hidden truths behind the things his daughter said.

"Where may I put my tools?" he asked. "I want to get started on my grandson's tree house before the storm arrives. And when can I meet the prisoner of Zenda?"

He'd told her often that a tree house should be built *before* a child's birth, in order to set that child's imagination on its course at once. He had also said often that a child's imagination came from other worlds—worlds she now believed in for the first time.

"He's not the prisoner of Zenda, Dad. I'm not usurping his throne," Ruby said.

Unless his throne was his house.

Her father had brought four bags of tools with him, plus a satchel containing a couple of changes of clothes. His hair was cut shorter than she remembered it, and had turned uniformly gray. It gave him the look that he'd been aiming for all of his life. Some would say he'd grown into himself, but they would be wrong. Before, he simply hadn't looked right.

"You can put your tools in my clinic. I've had hardly any patients since we opened it, and I already have the perfect tree picked out. But can we relax for half a minute first, Dad? Bob has been content for a couple of days, just sitting working on *Weir of Hermiston.*"

Bob. That he'd truly been Bob during those 'couple of days' had been difficult for her, for it was as if they had never met on the street, never had their weeks of love and intimacy. Except that he also knew that he was the father of her child.

"Weir is the name of a guy in his book," said Gerard, "and Hermiston is where Weir lives. If he wrote a book about me, he would have to call it *Gerard of Bank Street.*"

"If he wrote a book about me, it would be *Kenji of Kyushu* or *Kenji of Kyoto*," Ruby's father said. "It would not be *Kenji of Tacoma*, for that has been the easy part of my life."

"I wouldn't mind reading *Kenji of Kyushu* one of these days," said Ruby. "You never talk about your first couple of decades, Dad, what you might have been like as a child."

"If he wrote a book about Mr. Utterson—"

"Please now, Gerard," said Ruby. "My father's had a long flight."

It was true that his flight had been long and also delayed by the weather. But she knew that her father's ability to stand there making up book titles would equal Gerard's or anyone else's. There was a steadfast naïveté about him, a guilelessness like that which Mr. Utterson attributed to Gerard, that drew people in and somehow made its way into his art, though the art itself was anything but naïve.

"Do you want to see my room?" Gerard asked. "There's a pig poster in it. You can take a rest down there if you want to, and keep an eye on your tools at the same time. Though I don't think Bank Street has tool thieves."

"I'd rather rest in a room of my own," said Ruby's father. "But I wouldn't mind a cup of tea first. Tea, a rest, and then the tree house. See now, Ruby? I have also learned that things can sometimes wait."

"We have black tea and green tea and yellow tea with ginger in it," Gerard said. "We also have Nescafé Gold Blend freeze-dried coffee. . . ."

When her father said that he used to drink Nescafé Gold Blend freeze-dried coffee in Kyoto, Ruby took him into the parlor to sit with her on his couch, while Gerard ran off to the kitchen.

Was she going crazy, too, or did everyone have a period when Nescafé Gold Blend freeze-dried coffee played a part in their life?

Her father took a yellow *furoshiki* out of his clothing satchel, a *furoshiki* older than his daughter, and brought it with him into the parlor. It was wrapped around something thick and square and squat.

"I've brought your mother's Noh mask with me," he said. "Perhaps we could hang it in my grandson's room, where he will be able to feel her love."

Her mother's love was not her worry; that ship sailed when she was five years old. It was *her* love she worried about now . . . whether or not she would have it for an infant she'd created with a ghost.

Though she had recently bought a bassinet and crib, she hadn't given a thought about her baby's having a room of his own.

"You always said that Mom's mask was your only failure, Dad. But sure, we'll hang it above his crib. . . . Maybe a mother's love skips a generation, like certain genetic diseases that I studied about in school."

Always before, she'd been careful not to criticize her mother in his presence. What had changed now?

"I said that your mother's mask was one of my *many* failures, but it was also my only success," he said. "Without it, I would be lost."

He reached toward his crooked teapot on the coffee table, placing his index finger just beneath its ever-falling drop. It gave the impression that the drop would soon burst, making his finger wet. A dam was about to burst in the heavens above them, too, Ruby thought, washing out all of New York.

"But it is really true that you carved Mom into the mask *before* you met her, right?" Ruby asked. "That's not something you made up."

She had wanted to ask that question for years but never had. Something had changed in the fabric of her relationship with her father. Whether that meant it was torn or mended, however, she didn't know. She held her breath, waiting for his answer.

"Of course I didn't make it up. She was first in the mask, then in my life, and then she went back into the mask again," he said. "Your mother has never *not* been with me, Ruby. That is why my grief for her was never very difficult. . . ."

She wanted more than that and thought for a second he would give it to her, but he looked around and asked instead, "Where is my friend Guido? Do you remember the story of my tuxedo and his hair?"

"Guido has fur, not hair," said Gerard, back with a single cup of coffee. "And we don't want more coffee, do we, Dr. Okada? We had ours this morning."

"I should have said *fur*, but the story is the same either way," Ruby's father said.

"No, it's not the same, because dogs have hair and cats have fur," said Gerard, "and everyone knows that a story has to be told in a certain way. Stories have lives of their own!" He smiled a little sorrowfully, as if he were afraid that he might have hurt Ruby's father's feelings. "But that doesn't mean that I don't want to hear the story," he said. "I'm all ears, Ruby's dad!"

Though she could see he was perplexed, Ruby asked her father to go ahead with the story, while Gerard settled down on the piano bench, his chin resting in both of his palms.

"Some years ago, I came to New York for an opening at the Museum of Modern Art," her father said. "I was supposed to stand in front of my painting in my tuxedo, while other artists stood in front of theirs. Ruby was joining me at the opening, but she was slow to get ready. . . . Guido was a kitten back then, and Ruby had a couch he used to sleep on, which I slumped down upon while I waited for her. I thought her couch was clean, because it looked clean. That it was not was made clear when Ruby was finally ready and I stood to go to MoMA, only to find Guido's hair all over the back of my tuxedo."

"Guido's *fur*!" said Gerard.

Ruby's father blew across the top of his coffee. Steam came up, screening his expression behind it.

"It must have happened to others before me," he said, "but that was the first time I wore black on her couch, the first time I wore something dark enough, in other words, to turn the invisible visible. When I went into the bathroom, I had to take my tuxedo off and whack it out the window, Guido's *fur* floating off into the night. Then I found a vacuum cleaner cowering in Ruby's closet and vacuumed the couch for half an hour, with great balls of *fur* appearing on the vacuum cleaner's brush. . . . It made us late for MoMA, but it taught me to believe in the invisible worlds around us."

Gerard nodded politely, reluctant to say, after the hair and fur kerfuffle, that he believed in all the worlds, whether he could see them or not. And also that "great balls of fur," reminded him of "Great Balls of Fire," which he could play on the piano.

Chapter Ten

23

BOB WAS SINGING "Nice Work if You Can Get It," when they went up to his room early on the evening of Ruby's father's arrival. After having worked hard to clear brush from around the base of the tree-house tree for the last few hours, they were all quite dirty and exhausted. That the song Bob sang had been written some forty years after his death, no one seemed prepared to say.

Mr. Utterson, however, did say, "I don't know how nice it is, but it's necessary work. One can't build a tree house if there's detritus in the way."

"Detritus?" asked Ruby's father. "Is that like the leftover flotsam and jetsam after a ship goes down? I had two cats named Flotsam and Jetsam when I lived in Kyoto. One of the cats was furry, while the other was ugly and hairless."

He did not look at Gerard.

"*Detritus* means rubbish, waste, litter, scrap, the dregs of what society has to offer," said Bob. "It is also what's left when a writer writes poorly—it's the lies on those balled-up papers beneath a writer's desk."

"That's what happens when you tell a story the wrong way, too!" Gerard said. "A story should be told just right."

He didn't look at Ruby's father.

Ruby had hoped that Bob would be Archie by evening, since his writing was over for the day. There were no papers balled up under his desk, but otherwise his room had about as much detritus as the base of the tree house tree did, for though Bob cleaned it up each morning, along came someone else to knock it out of order every night. She suspected it was Archie himself, angry at the daily invasion. The only thing neat at the moment, in fact, *was* his desk, which had lined-up papers and pens.

"How are things going for poor Mr. Weir?" Gerard asked. "Are his neighbors any nicer to him now? You told me before that they were all pretty mean. Maybe he should move somewhere else."

"Well, his neighbors still frown at him from across the nave at his church; that much hasn't changed since I left him," said Bob. "But I can't seem to move the story forward from that point. . . ."

"Death has a way of limiting one's imagination. You have to be alive to write a really good story," Bette said. The expression on her face said, Why not cut to the chase?

"Death?" asked Ruby's father.

Bette came forward to stand beside him. Mr. Utterson stood by Ruby. This was farther than they'd dared to go before.

Bob peered grouchily at them. "Well, I'm not dead now," he said after giving it some thought. "What's the term for dead one minute, back to life the next?"

"*Fickle?*" asked Ruby's father, making Bob laugh.

"Fickle, yes, when one doesn't know what one truly cares about," he said. "It's a terrible state to be in. But surely there's a better word than that?"

"*Surprised?*" Gerard asked. "I know I would be surprised if I came back to life, but I think I'd be pretty happy about it."

"The biggest surprise about death for me was to learn that it's not everlasting," said Bob, "though that word came up often in the hymns I learned when I lived in New York in the winter of 1887."

He sang in a reedy voice, "*Leaning, leaning, safe and secure from all alarms; leaning / Leaning, leaning on the everlasting arms.* The Calvinists believed that 'everlasting arms' meant eternal life with Jesus, while I was inclined to think it meant to never again be bothered by life's pain. I can't speak for the Calvinists, but it looks like I was wrong."

"I know what *leaning* means," Gerard said. "It means not standing up straight." His own square body listed to the left.

"Why didn't you tell me all of this before? Or try to tell me, at least," said Ruby. "I might not have understood, but I could have gotten you some help."

This was why she longed for Archie, why she wished that he would never again be Bob. Because when Bob was here, her heart got broken again every time she came upstairs.

The anguished look she bore just then caused Mr. Utterson to try to take her hand.

"I didn't tell you because I believed, like many men do, that love conquers all," Bob said. "But as it's turned out, 'all' is too big a thing to conquer, even for love."

"Yet here you are now, wanting to finish a book you were writing when you died. Do I have that right?" asked Ruby's father. "If so, then that's not 'all'; it's just one thing. Do you suppose it means art can conquer love *and* death, that it's the work that counts and not the person who does it?"

There was his naïveté again. No matter how bizarre a thing

might be, or how absurd it might sound to others, he was simply asking a question.

"I don't *want* to finish my book; I *must* finish my book. But in my current state, I don't have the imagination for it, there's the rub. So perhaps you're right in saying that the work's more important than the man. Perhaps I ought to turn it over to someone else, someone who can imagine its ending better than I. With *Jekyll and Hyde,* with *Treasure Island* . . . even with *Kidnapped,* the words came pouring forth. But here I sit with Weir and Kirstie, no closer to ending their story than when I first began."

Ruby's father shrugged. "In my experience, it comes when it comes," he said. "A feeling akin to sickness comes over you, a wave of *knowing* that you can make a thing of beauty if you don't wait around. *That's* when you have to get to work."

"You're right!" Bob said. "The first half of Weir's story came roaring out from under the waving Samoan palms, but now my feet seem stuck in Scottish mud! God how I hate this waiting around!"

He lifted one foot and then the other. The foot attached to the leg he'd stabbed came lower off the floor.

"Maybe it's your wounded leg that hinders your imagination," Bette said. "Most people can't think straight when they're in pain."

He glared at her dismissively, but it was also clear that something in him shifted just then, which Ruby chalked up to her father's line of questioning. After all these days of everyone's trying to talk to this man, along came her father and talk flowed like rain.

"My leg is a pain in my ass," Bob grumbled. "Hand me a

cutlass and I'll lob the whole thing off, cast it down to Davy Jones. . . ."

Ruby's father bent down to peer into his eyes, a bit like an ophthalmologist might.

"We were talking about whether unfinished art dies with the artist, or wants its own completion no matter who completes it, as if it had a life of its own," he said. "It would help me a lot to know your opinion on that, since you seem to have a unique perspective."

"It does die with the artist," Bob said glumly. "That's why I can't finish my novel. I was only joking when I suggested turning it over to someone else."

"But if a spark came into you that *did* allow you to finish your novel, would you think differently than you do now?"

"I would," said Bob, "but no spark's coming."

"I ask because my father died before I was born—in fact, on an island not far from Samoa. He was an artist, like you, and what lived on after him in me was his art. I'm saying that his spark came into me and that yours might come back again in your son. That would be better than nothing, would it not?"

It was the most revealing thing that Ruby had ever heard her father say about his past.

"He was, Dad?" she asked. "My grandpa was an artist, too? I didn't know that. And he was killed on an island near Samoa? What was the island's name?"

"Guam," her father said. "Summer of 1944."

"So you were in your mother's body when your father died, just as this man's son is in your daughter's body now?" said Mr. Utterson.

He spoke as if he were summing something up in court, but Ruby didn't like it. Leave her son out of this.

"No one in my family was an artist before me," Bob said. "But I'm not comfortable with the term, for it draws attention to the self and not the work. Make no mistake, my only goal here is to set Weir free. If my son could do it . . . well, that's a thought I haven't had before, but that would be all right with me."

"I only use *artist* for convenience sake," said Ruby's father. "My point is, we should use whatever is at hand, and damn well get on with things."

"*Writer,* then," said Bob. "I'll call myself a writer who cannot write, a writer whose characters sit dumbly on their milking stools with no thoughts at all in their heads."

For the first time that evening, he looked directly at Ruby, but *her* only goal by then was to rescue her son's individuality.

"What was my grandfather's name, Dad?" she asked. "I've just now decided that I'd like to name my baby after him."

"I assumed you'd name him Robert, after *my* grandfather, famous in all of Scotland for his lighthouses," said Bob, his face taking on a pout.

"Yasuhiro," Ruby's father said. "In English, it means 'abundantly tranquil.' He wasn't cut out to be a soldier, even in his name. All he ever wanted, according to my mother, was to practice his *odori* and calligraphy."

"Abundant tranquillity is not a characteristic one wants in a writer, either," Bob said. "Robert, now . . ."

"Yasuhiro it is," said Ruby. "Maybe we'll call him Yasu for short."

"Might Robert be his middle name?" asked Bob. 'Yasuhiro Robert Stevenson . . .' Can't finish my book, can't get my son named after my own sweet grandfather . . ."

"Stop," said Ruby. "His name will be Yasuhiro Robert

Billingsly. Whichever dead ancestor might want to shoot sparks of the artist into him, we'll use the family name of the man who shot the sperm."

She had brought her mother's Noh mask with her, wrapped back up in its ancient yellow *furoshiki*. She'd intended to leave it in the crib in her bedroom but had carried it up here by mistake. When she began to unwrap it, the others got quiet.

"Would you like to meet my mother, Bob?" she asked. "She will be on guard against anyone messing with her grandson."

"A fear of every Scot is having to meet his mother-in-law," Bob said.

In a fuguelike state of her own by then, what with her current fears and all the revelations about her father's father, Ruby picked the Noh mask up and put it to her face. It was hard and cold against her lips and forehead, not in the least a pleasant sensation, but when she looked through its long and narrow eye slits, the scene before her grew focused. Gerard's skin had a bluish tinge, as if his kindness were showing through, as did, to a lesser degree, Mr. Utterson's. Bette's breasts looked smaller, her eyes looked larger, and Ruby's father's entire face seemed swallowed up by his open mouth.

But though Bob at first seemed only put off by the mask, as if believing it to be another intrusion, when she continued to stare at him through it, when she wouldn't look away, his face flipped back into a fearful Archie's, quite as if he were taking his Bob mask down at the command of Ruby's mother's mask. And then he said something that changed the course of everything to that point. . . .

"Great-Grandmother, may I play with my train now?" he asked. "I've recited both books, with no mistakes in either one."

Ruby wanted to search for the train but was afraid to look away from him now. "Recited both books?" she said. "Let me hear the last few lines of one of them, then, so I can be sure that you're not lying."

She dared not look at anyone else, or give any thought to what she was doing. Archie, however, simply closed his eyes and spoke in a youthful voice: "*Oxen and wain-ropes would not bring me back again to that accursed island; and the worst dreams that ever I have are when I hear the surf booming about its coasts, or start upright in bed, with the sharp voice of Captain Flint still ringing in my ears: "Pieces of eight! Pieces of eight!"*"

"Not bad," said Ruby's mother's mask, "but tell me who is speaking."

"Why, it's Young Jim Hawkins, of course, you know that, Great-Grandmother," Archie said. "He tells the story from its start until its end."

"Come on, Dr Okada, let him play with his train now. That was the deal," said Gerard.

As he spoke, he and Mr. Utterson went looking for the train, which lay in the corner off its tracks, as if derailed.

'Not so fast," the mask said. "Give me the other book's ending, too. To say the ending of one correctly might simply be dumb luck. If you want to play with your train once, you've got to earn it twice. That is my new rule."

Her father now joined Gerard and Mr. Utterson in setting the electric train up.

"But it's the longest ending," said Archie. "And though I didn't make mistakes before, I might make one now."

"Longest ending?" Ruby's mother's mask growled.

It was like someone from Dickens growling, "More?"

Tears came into Archie's eyes, but he knew better than to wait any longer.

"About a week has passed, and I am now finishing this statement under the influence of the last of the old powders. This, then, is the last time, short of a miracle, that Henry Jekyll can think his own thoughts or see his own face (now how sadly altered!) in the glass. Nor must I delay too long to bring my writing to an end; for if my narrative has hitherto escaped destruction, it has been by a combination of great prudence and great good luck. Should the throes of change take me in the act of writing it, Hyde will tear it in pieces; but if some time shall have elapsed after I have laid it by, his wonderful selfishness and circumscription to the moment will probably save it once again from the action of his ape-like spite. And indeed the doom that is closing on us both, has already changed and crushed him. . . ."

"Okay, enough," said Ruby, "skip to the very last sentence."

"Here then, as I lay down the pen and proceed to seal up my confession, I bring the life of that unhappy Henry Jekyll to an end."

He looked at her pleadingly, hopeful and exhausted.

Ruby didn't have to ask who the speaker was this time, nor whom Archie thought he'd been talking to, for she felt the grip of Anna Stevenson Billingsly take firm hold of her chest.

Chapter Eleven

24

ALL THREE ANNA STEVENSON BILLINGSLY photographs sat like billboards, each at a turn of Archie's train track, while Ruby's mother's Noh mask sat atop a box at turn number four.

In the hours since Archie's book recitations, Ruby's father and the others had fixed the electric train and set it up, complete with bridges over a blue plastic river, an automobile signal crossing, and a dock with a hydraulic arm, where coal might be loaded into coal cars. Since Archie didn't have any coal, he shredded the newer pages of *Weir of Hermiston* with no hesitation at all, despite Gerard's caution that Bob might not like it when he got back.

"That's his problem," said Archie. "All he ever does is sit around and write. And who knows? Maybe he won't come back for once. Some people just don't know when they've worn out their welcome."

Ruby and Bette stood stewing—now that the dam had burst, everything was happening too fast—while Mr. Utterson crawled around the track with a tiny oil can, squirting drops of oil onto every moving part. He'd found a few old railroad caps, too, and wore one on his head. Archie, meanwhile, peered through the engine's window at the toy engineer, whose elbow rested on the window's ledge.

"All aboard!" he called once or twice.

"It makes no sense," said Ruby. "Look at my mother's mask, and then at any of these Anna Stevenson Billingsly photos, and you see absolutely no resemblance, yet he crumbled under the weight of her stare in about two minutes."

"Oh, I don't know," Bette said. "I think she looks a little like the middle-aged Anna—wooden expression, terrible fucking haircut."

In the box with the railroad caps, Gerard had discovered a couple dozen toy railroad passengers and workers—the passengers in holiday clothing, the workers in various uniforms. He stuck those with bent legs through the train car's windows and onto little bench seats, and stationed the workers strategically: the conductor on the platform, looking at his watch; a man with a shovel in his hands lodged between the engine and the coal car; the ticket taker ready for the passengers whose legs weren't bent . . . who were, by then, lined up.

"Where is this train going, and what's its name?" he asked.

Gerard wore a railroad cap, too, as did Ruby's father, though it made him look like a Japanese infantryman from World War II. Perhaps he looked like his own father had, before getting killed on Guam.

"Most of the time it's the Edinburgh-London express, but I like it better when it's a local," said Archie, "for then I get to call out the station names. It's stopped in Cambridge now 'cause that's where it broke down."

"He's just a boy at play with other boys," Bette said. "I'll bet he didn't get to do that much during his actual childhood. What we need to try to do now is take him from this age and—"

"Bring him up to speed?" asked Mr. Utterson, popping up next to them and smiling. He had that tiny oil can resting in his hand. As he spoke, he kept his eyes on Bette's *OMG AKA WTF* slogan, stretched across her breasts again. It had been Bette's idea to place the Anna Stevenson Billingsly photos around the train tracks, and he had backed her up. She had wanted to place the Archie photos there, too, but Ruby had not allowed it. And now Ruby stepped away from them in order to speak directly to Archie. She supposed she wanted to take a page out of Bette's book and strike while the iron was hot.

"During the time you've been waiting here in Cambridge, what have you learned about the place?" she asked. "Can you tell me something I don't know? The river that flows beneath that bridge over there, for example . . . can you tell me its name?"

She tried to sound casual but winced at the clumsiness of her questions.

"It's the Cam, of course," said Archie, happy to be of service.

He pointed at his railroad bridge and the blue plastic river beneath it. "Where the Cam has a bridge, you find the town," he said. "They like to joke that the town is full of dons and the river is full of swans. Here's a riddle I learned: Why does the Cam have shells when it doesn't have oysters or clams?"

"I give up," said Ruby. "I like riddles, but that's a hard one."

"I give up, too," said Gerard.

He had pulled his railroad cap from his head in order to scratch his scalp.

"It has shells because men row in them," Archie told them.

Gerard didn't get it, but he smiled and smiled.

25

THINGS WENT WELL OVER THE COURSE of that night and for most of the next day, at least in so far as Archie continuing to be Archie was concerned. Bette would occasionally ask him to recite different passages from *Treasure Island* or *Dr. Jekyll and Mr. Hyde*, but no matter which passages she chose, no matter how obscure, he recited them willingly and well, neither afraid of her asking nor missing even so much as a comma pause.

They continued to stay with him in four-hour shifts and in pairs, usually Bette and Ruby's father, or Gerard and Mr. Utterson, all while New York shut down, with subways stopping, people evacuating low-lying areas, and waves rattling Rockaway Beach and lower Manhattan. The others tried to order Ruby to stay in her room, not only because of Hurricane Sandy but also because her baby's due date was nearly upon them. Archie sometimes slept, of course, and when he did, they did also, on the floor beside his bed, or out on the landing, or down in Ruby's father's bedroom.

What came clear to Ruby and Bette over those hours was not only what should have been obvious from the beginning—that the abuse leveled at Archie the child had planted mutant seeds in the formative tissues of his psyche, but also that his great-grandmother's demands had had the unexpected by-product of giving him any number of portals through which he could slip, wearing the clothing and using the language of any character he chose. Thus, old Ben Gunn could ask Gerard for cheese; Dr. Livesey might give his opinion on Ruby's pregnancy; and that astonishing amalgam, Henry **HYDE**, could rain havoc down on a hapless true believer like Mary Andrew Michaelsonsen.

Whether Archie did this knowingly or unknowingly, that was the question. And the other question was, how, from that stinking witch's brew, had he managed to summon Bob, with all Bob's wit and memories intact?

26

AND THEN, LATE ON THAT SECOND DAY, Ruby's father let it be known that he wanted to go out into the approaching storm.

Three weeks before his arrival in New York, he told them, he had gone online to buy himself a ticket (two tickets, actually) for the reopening and rededication of the Statue of Liberty, scheduled for October 28, after a year of closure for repairs. It was something that he desperately wanted to see. The original dedication of the statue had been October 28, 1886—it was its 126th anniversary—so though the wind howled and rain lashed everyone who dared to go outside, *and* though his grandson was due at any minute, he prepared to head on down to Battery Park in order to take the fifteen-minute ferry ride. Had the statue's grand opening been postponed, he would have stayed home, of course, but his belief in the wisdom of those who made such decisions was unwavering, and yet another example of his naïveté.

"Don't worry, it's as safe as can be," he told Ruby. "I'll be back in a couple of hours, three at the most, and, in any case, in time for my next shift with Archie."

That he'd bought the second ticket for her, ridiculous as that seemed now, he kept to himself. Before he left, however, and in the face of her growing incredulousness, he did say one other thing.

"When I told Archie where I was going and told him the

original dedication date, he asked if he could go with me, really almost begged," he said. "I told him no. I said I couldn't take him, but he asked with such passion, Ruby, and then he said one other thing, which I can't leave without telling."

They were standing in the vestibule, wind so rattling the frame of the front door that it seemed like the rising music in a movie.

"Just go, Dad," she said. "The sooner you get out of here, the sooner you'll get back."

This had been her ploy since childhood—to refuse to let him tell her what he thought was so important.

This time, however, the ploy didn't work, for he put up the hood on his rain slicker and stepped outside.

Oh, what was the one other thing that Archie had said?

Ruby nearly ran after him.

Chapter Twelve

27

RUBY'S FATHER: *She often said she was happy with me, that she wasn't always wretched. But then her wretchedness descended again, coming out of nowhere.*

RUBY: *It's true that unhappiness can't always be kept at bay, but are you suggesting that even such a joyous moment as my birth couldn't penetrate her depression?*

RUBY'S FATHER: *She used to have a bruise on her forehead above her right eye, a "pall" I guess you'd call it, and that is in the mask, as well. When I carved it, I thought it was a blemish in the wood, and then I thought it wasn't, for it wasn't always there.*

RUBY: *Perhaps it was God's early warning system, working like a lighthouse in reverse, warning of a rot inside.*

RUBY'S FATHER: *But the worry I have now is this: If she wasn't happy to see you when you were born, if that pall brought a curtain down, isn't it possible that you won't be happy to see your son, whose birth will be upon us shortly?*

When Ruby awoke from her nap, after dreaming that conversation with her father, it was four hours later and he still had not returned, had missed the beginning of his next shift with Archie.

She rose and turned to look for Guido and Francesca, both of whom sat across her bedroom from here, in the armchair beside the telescope, side by side and staring out at the ferocious storm. Water was rising everywhere. All of New York would soon be under it, and her father might be, as well. Why he wasn't back yet and why he hadn't called, she didn't know, nor did she have the slightest idea why she would have dreamed of her mother at a time like this. She should have been dreaming of Archie or Bob. She should have dreamed a dream in which *somebody* told her what the last thing Archie had said to her father was.

She stood and went to sit on the ottoman, in front of the terrified animals, and once more closed her eyes, she supposed in order to keep herself from seeing Hurricane Sandy destroy them. Hearing it would be enough. If her father wasn't back in fifteen more minutes, she would call 911.

In Tacoma, during her childhood, Ruby's tree house ladder had caused her endless problems. Not after she was in the tree house—then all she had to do was pull the ladder up—but on those long summer evenings when her father called her back inside—then it dangled dangerously down, inviting any stranger to climb up. She used to assign herself guard duty at her bedroom window, on the lookout for invaders, but she always fell asleep before they came. And against all odds, she fell back asleep now, as well, to the sounds of rain lashing against the side of her house, and with worry about her father put on hold.

Where are you, Bob? she asked in a new dream. *Why don't you talk to me and not my father? Why don't I get to hear whatever you have to say that's so important?*

As she spoke, Bob came climbing awkwardly down that dangling rope ladder from her childhood tree house. He was wearing his Scottish tweeds, and carrying a flask of single malt.

Because I don't know what you need me for, he said, *when hearing it from your father works just as well.*

That cast her speechless. How could he say such a thing? What did she need him for? She needed him so that they could talk about their child, of course. And, though it seemed farcical now, so that they could also talk about what once had passed for love.

Why are you here, then, if you don't know even that much? she asked. *What good are you if I can always get my father to interpret what you say? He translated my mother's true feelings about me in that other dream I just had, so I'm sure he can translate yours, as well.*

As you wish, said Bob. *I only came because you called me. But my love for you was never false.*

He gave her an exasperated look, as if saying, How could you not know that?

It was every bit as false as you were, she said. *But what I want now is, for once in your life, for you to talk to me plainly. I'm tired of always having the weight of that put on me! With all that's going on, it really is a matter of life and death.*

Now that you mention it, I'm fond of conversations about life and death, Bob said after a second or two. *We can talk about that if you like.*

I meant that what we do next might be *a matter of life and death for one of us . . . for Archie or me or our son. . . . But okay, what do you have to say about life and death? Does your current state give you a better idea of what's what with that? Do the dead know more about death than the living know about life? It hardly seems that they could know less.*

She felt a little release just then, could suddenly breathe more fully. But when he said, *Beats me. I'm not dead now, and when I was, I didn't think about it,* her breath grew tight again. There was no hope in talking to this man. Hope might come only from having him leave her alone forever.

I've tried my best to understand you. . . . tried my best to understand myself when I am with you, but all you ever do is speak in clever ways. I've had enough. Beats you, you say? Well, having you come into my life like this has beaten me. What are you even doing here? Why did you come to torment Archie, and why are you tormenting me?

Come on, he said. *Don't give up so easily. I'll do what you asked. I'll talk plainly now, if only you will listen with your ears properly open.*

She kept her lips pursed but looked up at him with her head cocked. This was the entreaty that had besotted him from the beginning, from the moment they met by that elevator. She could no longer recall what had so besotted her—except for those far-apart eyes.

Do you know how scientists have trouble explaining our need for sleep? he asked. *And do you know how pleasant sleep is at its deepest, when we're aware enough to appreciate it but can't reflect on that appreciation?*

She nodded and opened her eyes for a second on the ottoman. The storm had petrified the dog and cat. She closed her eyes again, and willed him to finish his point.

Well, the closest I can come to answering your question about death is to say that it's a lot like that. It's a floating tub of warmth and kindness, and it's got a certain buoyancy about it.

She hadn't intended to ask him a question about death; she had meant it as a metaphor for saying that matters were urgent.

Who hasn't equated death to sleep? she huffed. *There's nothing new in that.*

There's nothing new in anything that I might have to say, he said. *I am only telling you how I got here as clearly as I can. I was nodding away in the lake I've just described, dreamless but also happy, when suddenly . . .*

He stopped and put his hands out, palms up.

Hey, it's raining even harder than it was before. . . . Fifteen minutes have passed by now, yet your father's still not yet back. Don't you think it's time you made that 911 call?

Forget my father! said Ruby. *You were nodding away in that lake when suddenly what?*

When suddenly I heard Archie crying. His cries woke me up.

She sensed that he was about to climb into her childhood tree again, but he started disappearing from the bottom up, like Dodgson's cat.

Come on, Bob! When suddenly what?

When suddenly I found myself here as His emissary. Once in a while he feels a little something for us. He isn't always paring his nails.

At his emphasis on *always,* he disappeared completely, and she found herself awake but not alone on that ottoman.

Guido and Francesca had climbed into her lap.

Chapter Thirteen

28

"Really? He said 'emissary'? He said '*He,*' like in God? Are you kidding me? He said '*He* isn't always pairing his nails?' What is this, Ruby, dreams of Christianity 101?"

"I guess," said Ruby. "I suppose I could have pretended he said 'She,' modernizing things a bit."

She felt good, ready for whatever the day might bring, and she wasn't about to let Bette's sarcasm wear her down. "Anyway, it was in my dream; it isn't as if he actually said it. Happy Halloween, by the way."

"Happy Halloween," said Bette, "and happy almost birthday whatshisname? Hiro, is it?"

"Yasuhiro Robert, but I'm fading a bit on the Billingsly. Maybe Yasuhiro Robert Okada. I told my dad that that would be his name when he finally got home. And after I convinced myself not to kill him."

"He's something else, that father of yours, venturing out into the storm of the decade just to visit the Statue of Liberty. . . . If he were ten years younger, you'd be calling me 'stepmother' by the end of the year. And there is no blemish on the forehead of that mask he made, either, by the way. While he was gone, I checked it out. Your mother or not your mother, she looks like the fucking Avon lady."

The order of their Archie shifts had changed during Ruby's father's absence, and had stayed changed since, with Gerard and Mr. Utterson doing most of the work, while Ruby's father caught up on his sleep and Bette got ready to go to the hospital for the post Hurricane Sandy cleanup. It was October 31; subways and trains were starting to run again and airplanes were starting to fly.

Ruby's father had stayed in his room all of October 30 and most of today. He wasn't gone for less than four hours, but for slightly over twenty-four.

"You know what else we have to remember to do, whether Yasuhiro comes today or not, is help Gerard go trick-or-treating tonight," Ruby said. "He's got his bag; he knows the drill. . . . Mr. Utterson had his Mark Twain suit dry-cleaned for the Village Halloween parade, but now that it's canceled, he's wearing it anyway, he says, to make the people in our neighborhood happy. We should buy some candy for the other trick-or-treaters, too, if there are any."

"Yeah," said Bette. "As if we don't have freaks enough *inside* this house. . . ."

Bette had been in Ruby's bedroom with her, helping her pack a maternity bag, which she zipped up now in order to walk ahead of Ruby with it, down to the first floor. While Ruby was in the bath that morning, Bette had also set up Yasuhiro's crib, put sheets and blankets on its new mattress and attached a pretty mobile—chicks and geese and ducks—ready to dance like sugarplums above the baby's head.

No doubt because it was the only room she'd furnished herself, Ruby preferred the parlor to the living room, which held the Billingsly library, complete with family scrapbooks and a bookcase dedicated to Bob's two memorized novels, some copies old and dog-eared, others that had never been opened. But though she preferred the parlor, she asked Bette to go into the living room with her now in order to help her drag her mother's braided rug out to the hallway, where she intended to do her breathing exercises in that grid of overlapping light. She'd been deeply worried about her father when he was gone, and needed to feel that tension flow out of her. She was sure that her baby would be born today, and that after that things would be all right.

While they were in the living room, Bette pulled back the curtain and stared out into the bleak and overcast street. "Look," she said, "that creepy woman's here again. Never mind the gloomy weather, Ruby, I think she's about to start singing 'On the Street Where You Live.'"

Ruby had seen Mary Andrew Michaelsonsen a few times lately, too, dodging in and out of the wind gusts, but she didn't think of her as creepy—rather, she thought of her as lovesick, forlorn . . . betrayed, as Ruby had been, by the world's most bizarre set of circumstances. . . . Or, worse than that, by death come to life again.

"Maybe we should call the soup kitchen. Let them know she's here," said Bette. "We don't need Liza Doolittle hanging around right now."

"Eliza Doolittle was *inside* Henry Higgins's house," Ruby said, but when she went to stand by Bette, she lost her light-heartedness. Mary Andrew looked as abject as the street around her, like she'd been torn from the pages, not of a book by Bob, but from one about debtors' prisons. "Lets *do* call the soup kitchen," she said. "We've got to get her surrounded by people who love her."

"Or can stand being around her, at least," said Bette.

29

As THE DAY WORE ON, Mary Andrew disappeared again, Mr. Utterson made them all a fine English lunch, and Ruby's father, nervous and disheveled, came downstairs to sit at the parlor piano and play and sing "Happy, Happy Birthday Baby," by The Tune Weavers, a song that he had loved when he was young and easy in Kyoto. He sang it like the blues, not like the doo-wop song it had been, but when he got to the line about spoiling someone's birthday, he stopped, patted the piano bench beside him, and waited until Ruby came in from the hallway, where she'd been watching him.

"I hope you're singing that for Yasuhiro," she said. "And spoil his birthday? My God, Dad, for a while I thought you might deprive him of the only grandfather he's got left. What were you thinking, staying out all night long like that?"

When he started singing again—about remembering the love they had for each other—she sat, put her hands on his, pulled them off the keyboard, and closed the lid of the piano. Its mirrored finish reflected their shoulders and heads. She looked like a misshapen balloon, he like *The Scream*, by Edvard Munch.

"I remember the love *we* had for each other perfectly well," she said. "And in honor of that love, I need an explanation. You came here to help me, but all you've done since you got here is freak me out, Dad. Okay, you're building a tree house, and I appreciate it, but you brought that despicable mask—surely you know that it's terrified me since I was a child—and you ran off into an outside storm, when the inside storm was nearly causing me to have a nervous breakdown. "

He moved his hands back up to rest them on the piano lid. "Nervous breakdown?" he asked. "Is that the medical definition of it?"

"Come on, Dad, spill. What happened out at the Statue of Liberty or down at Battery Park, or wherever the hell you were for all those hours? Why didn't you come home?"

She remembered trying to get Bob to talk straight to her in her dream. . . . This felt a lot like the same thing.

"I like the idea that a 'nervous breakdown' is what the entire northeast region of the United States had during that storm," he said. "It makes me feel that nature and human nature are really just two sides of the same coin."

That was *so* like him! It was the kind of thing he always said, and he almost always got away with it. Not this time, though. This time, she wanted answers, not some polemic he invented in order to keep himself hidden.

"Bette's enamored of you," she said. "She's new to these tricks of yours, Dad, thinks they're charming. Not me, though. So let me paraphrase her here: 'Spill the fucking beans.' What happened to you, and why were you gone for so long?"

"I had no trouble getting to the ferry terminal, but I had two Statue of Liberty tickets, remember, so I thought I might sell the other one. I stood a little off from where people were getting in line and held it up like hawkers do outside of sports stadiums. Occasionally, I said, 'Extra ticket, no extra charge,' so they wouldn't think I was a scalper, but the wind and rain made people hurry by me as if I weren't there. No one slowed down or even looked my way, though my ticket was for the day's last ferry and the ticket windows had already closed. I was irritated, and getting soaking wet."

Ruby kept her eyes on his face in the closed lid of the piano, where it now seemed as if the man from *The Scream* were telling her this story.

"Soon I saw a group of brand-new citizens, people who, their guide announced, had taken the oath of citizenship just that morning. So I stopped saying 'No extra charge' and started saying 'No charge at all. Welcome to America; the ferry ride's on me.' But even then they walked like ducks behind their guide, eyes looking straight ahead. Not one of them glanced toward me."

"They probably already had their tickets," Ruby said.

"No doubt they did, so when another group came by, I tried them. They were not new citizens, but Frenchmen and Frenchwomen dressed in nineteenth-century clothing and following a sign that said 'Dedication of the Statue of Liberty, October 28, 1886.' The sign was in French and the people following it were speaking French."

"'*Dédicace de la Statue de la Liberté, le 28 Octobre, 1886,*'" said Ruby. She had studied French all during high school and college, and still sometimes read novels in it. And once she'd had a truly dissociative patient who spoke French half the time.

Now she stopped staring at the keyboard lid, and when she looked directly at her father, she saw that his eyes were as narrow as the Noh mask's eye slits.

"Did they ignore you, too, the French people, or take your extra ticket off your hands?"

"They ignored me, too, but I soon discovered that they were part of an organized something or other—what do you call it when people pretend to be from another place and time?—and that to stop and talk to me would have ruined both their pretense and the timing of their march."

"A reenactment? Like people do with Civil War battles and at Renaissance fairs and such?"

"Yes, that's it! They were part of a reenactment. The French led the way, since they gave the Statue of Liberty to America, but they were followed by Italians, with their own sign, and Irishmen and Poles and Russian Jews, even Chinese . . . plus some other, smaller groups, with each group in costume and pretending in everything they did and said that it really was October 28, 1886."

"So who did you finally give your extra ticket to, and what happened after that to keep you away from home for an entire night and extra day?"

"Do you remember what I was asked to do with my extra ticket?" he asked. "I mean, after I understood that you would not be able to go with me."

"Of course I do. Archie wanted you to take him out into the storm. You also said that there was something else you had to tell me, but I got irritated and wouldn't listen to you."

It still made her angry to think about that, and it showed again in her voice.

"Well, the last group of whatever you call them—I guess *reenactors* would be the term—were Scots, all dressed up in kilts and such, though rain pelted their legs and soaked their high socks.

"There were four of them, one carrying a bagpipe he wanted to play when they got to Liberty Island, two carrying books that were published in 1886, and one with a bottle of very old whiskey, which he didn't want to share with the other three. That man, however, didn't have a ticket. He was preparing to wave to the others when the ferry left the dock, so he gladly shared his whiskey with me when I offered him my extra ticket."

"So that's what happened, then. You got drunk with four Scotsman. But how come it took all night?"

Her father looked at her like she had missed the point of his story entirely, sighed, and said, "That thing I wanted to tell you? Do you still not know what it was? And will you still refuse to hear it if I try to tell you again right now?"

"I won't refuse to hear it," Ruby said. "I shouldn't have refused to hear it before."

"It was absolutely 1886 when I joined those four Scotsmen and the other reenactors for the trip out to Liberty Island, and it was still 1886 when, one short hour later, we got back to Battery Park. The last trip of the day was cut short because of Hurricane Sandy, you see, and they were upset by that. The bagpiper was upset because no one could hear him through the noise of the storm, and those carrying books—now listen to me, Ruby—those carrying books were upset because there was no Statue of Liberty official available for them to present them to, as examples of the literature that Scots had published *in the year 1886.*"

"Holy shit," said Ruby. "*Dr. Jekyll and Mr. Hyde!*"

"Not only that but *Kidnapped* also," said her father. "Both of them published, in one way of looking at it, by the man we are keeping in that room upstairs, and both in the original Statue of Liberty year. Now here's what I think, though I didn't think it before I left the house. It wasn't exactly Archie who asked to go with me, but that growing tapeworm who lives within him, whose name I dare not say.

"By the time we got back to Battery Park, it was raining cats and dogs, so we repaired to a nearby Scottish pub by the name of Deacon Brodie, which was closed to all but my four Scotsmen and me, where all night long, while the storm raged and bellowed on the other side of the door, they never broke character, but drank and drank and pretty soon stood on stools and on the bar to read, *in their entirety*, those two books of your own baby's father." He paused, then added, "Can you imagine what storms might have raged inside that pub if I had taken him with me?"

"No," said Ruby, "I cannot."

"It has made me come to a conclusion about what is going on with that man, which I will share with you after I eat some of the lunch Mr. Utterson prepared. I drank too much and slept too much, and now I'm starving."

"What conclusion, Dad?" asked Ruby. "Tell me now or forever hold your peace."

It was that same old ploy of hers again, and it didn't work this time, either.

"Okay, then," she said before he left the room. "Go ahead and tell me later."

Chapter Fourteen

30

OVER THE COURSE OF THE REST of that day, when too much time went by, some of them started making bets. Yasuhiro would be born at two or three or four that afternoon. . . . He would be born at five, or precisely when it was dark enough for Gerard to join the mass of straggling poststorm trick-or-treaters.

As each hour passed, Ruby's mood changed from one of calm waiting—sure her baby's birth would be today and in the meantime thinking about her father's stirring story—to one of slight impatience: Okay, he would be born today, but *when* today?—to a resignation that, never mind how sure she'd been, her baby would not come out on his due date.

She rested on her parlor couch or sat cross-legged on her braided rug, doubly mindful of the fact that it was the only thing she owned that her mother had actually made, braided, she supposed, while deciding whether or not to succumb to the draw of that blemish, that pall.

As almost always happened, however, when she tried to think more deeply about her mother, her father invaded her thoughts. With Bette or Mr. Utterson or Gerard, Ruby had no trouble expressing herself, but with her father she could not, and the time they'd had early today was a prime example of that. They never had any trouble listening to music together or watching old movies and speaking about them when they were done. They could take sides on some intellectual issue, sawing through its thickness like lumberjacks on opposite sides of a log, but they appeared never to be able to simply sit and talk, for it always seemed to be her doing the sitting, and him doing the talking.

That was what she was thinking about when her father came downstairs after taking another nap, and said, "Tick, tock, Ruby. What is that song you used to sing that's got 'tick, tock' in it?"

Ruby was still on her rug, a Billingsly scrapbook on the floor beside her and another one open on her lap. She was once more trying to get to the bottom of Archie while she waited for her son. But she had loved the song her father was referring to and had sung it for him whenever he'd asked, which was often.

"My grandfather's clock was too large for the shelf / So it stood ninety years on the floor; / It was taller by half than the old man himself, / Though it weighed not a pennyweight more."

When she smiled at him, he sat down beside her. She admired his ability to sit cross-legged without any effort at all. She hoped that he would tell her the conclusions he had come to that morning without her having to ask again.

"'A watched clock never boils' was how your mother used to put it whenever you were waiting for something," he said.

"'A watched clock never boils' . . . Yes, I remember that."

She feared he would say, as he always used to, that it was supposed to be "watched pot," but this time he did not. He simply touched her abdomen, the veins on the back of his hand like underground tunnels. He seemed fully rested now, fully himself again, no longer carrying the weight of those four Scotsmen.

"I found these scrapbooks a while ago, each of them dedicated to one of those earlier Archies," she said. "A lot of care has gone into them; you might say a lot of love. She must have put them together herself."

She didn't have to tell him who "she" was.

"Which one is our Archie's father's and which is his grandfather's?" her father asked.

Oh, what conclusions had he come to, and were they different from her own?

"Archie S. is his grandfather. Archie O., if he'd lived, would be about your age now, Dad."

Since Ruby held the Archie O. Billingsly scrapbook, her father picked up Archie S.'s. After that, they spent time looking through them, both lost in the books they held.

Ruby was pleased to discover that Archie O. Billingsly had been athletic throughout high school. There were pictures of him running track—his best time in the mile, four minutes, thirty-nine seconds.

"How old would the Archie you've got there be if he'd lived, Dad?" she asked. "I forgot what his dates were on the photograph."

But her father was reading a letter he had found, not pasted in, but stuck in the back of the scrapbook, and didn't answer her question for a moment. Presently, however, he said, "He'd be almost as old as the man in the clock song, just like *my* father would have been if he had survived the war."

"Your father who was killed by the Americans?" she asked.

It made them both smile at the absurdity of saying it like that. She couldn't help thinking of those four Scotsman, stuck back in 1886.

Her father shook the letter he'd been reading until a leaf or two fell out of it. "This man's name was John McCormick. He wrote to Archie's mother after her son's death on the island of Guam," he said. "Guam, Ruby . . . where my father was killed, also."

"Let me see it," Ruby said, but he held the letter close to him.

"*My* mother got one of these, too, from a certain Major Nakamura," he said. "Major Nakamura came to our house once, when I was seven years old."

He opened his hand until the rest of John McCormick's letter fell out of it. Ruby picked it up and read aloud: "'Neither can I truthfully say that his death was an easy one. I only know from the bitter experience of having been wounded twice myself, once severely in action, that in the stress and excitement of battle there is no pain. . . .'"

She felt like she was eavesdropping, and put the letter down. She could not help thinking, never mind her training, that everything in the world, everything and every *time*, was intricately connected.

"Why did Major Nakamura go to your house, Dad?" she asked. "And what did his letter say about your father?"

"Only that my father was not a kamikaze, which was odd, because there were no kamikaze until later in the war. When Major Nakamura visited, he brought useful items from a store he owned—packages of Calpis, which kept well without refrigeration, lotions and toilet paper. . . . He wore his hat down low on his head, with its brim turned up at the front. He took me to a neighborhood park while my mother unpacked his gifts. He seemed to want to impart something important to me."

Ruby flashed her eyes down to the page of John McCormick's letter that was closest to her:

> *I can recall most vividly the long watches we stood together on a lonely outpost on Emirau. We would sit down on either side of the machine gun, and take turns staring into the darkness that shrouds the Pacific in the hours after midnight. Below us we could hear the restless tide lapping as it must have lapped for an infinity on these changing shores.*

"John McCormick wrote well," she said. "His words make me feel like we are also sitting beside that machine gun on Emirau. They make me feel that we all experience everything, Dad. Maybe that's what Major Nakamura wanted to impart. Does it sound strange for me to suggest that he wanted to tell you something like that?"

"I've never heard of Emirau, but no, it doesn't sound strange," her father said.

He smiled and reached over John McCormick's letter to settle a hand down on Ruby's abdomen. He loved to touch his coming grandson. She thought that this would be the moment that he told her what conclusions he had come to.

"What did Major Nakamura say?" she asked when he was quiet for a while. "It's funny you remember that his hat was pulled down."

"I remember his hat, but when I try to see his face, I see only the face of the actor Shimura Takashi, from the Kurosawa film *Ikiru*, singing about how life is short. I think the film came out that same year."

"Not in 1886?" she nearly said.

When Yasuhiro kicked, her father pulled his hand away again.

"Major Nakamura told me that my father asked him twice to be excused from the war," he said. "Once when Major Nakamura took command of the squadron, and again on the morning of my father's final day."

He picked up a page of John McCormick's letter and read: "'Perhaps the pain of your loss will be blunted till only a dim and hallowed memory remains. The memory of a man perhaps no braver, perhaps no more afraid than the rest who lived and loved and passed into the dim boundlessness of eternity. I do not know whether Archie Billingsly was brave, nor do I know the conflicting emotions that must have been running through his mind as they were running through the minds of every one of us that day. I know only that he fought well, fought with a clear mind and a clear conscience.'"

"Why do you keep reading, Dad? Why won't you tell me what else Major Nakamura said?" And also what conclusions you have come to . . .

"I keep reading because, by doing so, I *am* telling you what he said. That he didn't know whether my father was brave; that conflicting emotions ran through my father's heart; that time would blunt the pain I felt . . . But I never knew my father, so I had no need for time."

"This letter was to Anna Stevenson Billingsly. Are you simply saying that all such soldiers' letters are the same?"

"I am saying that all I wanted to do in the park that evening was play with the other children, not sit talking to a man with his hat pulled down," said her father. "Major Nakamura soon saw my disinterest and said 'Go play,' and sat in a park swing by himself. "

"And now you wish you'd shown more interest? I know how you felt. When someone tries to tell you something, you probably ought to listen to them. Maybe Major Nakamura's still alive. If we go to Japan together someday soon, we can always try to find him."

"You were five years old when your mother died," said her father. "Do you ever wish you knew more about her desire to be excused from life?"

"Come on, Dad. How can you say she wanted to be excused from life when she died of cardiac arrest?"

Quite suddenly, Yasuhiro kicked a couple of sharp times, and when she bent toward the pain, her father didn't say what she knew he was about to—that her mother's heart had arrested itself.

Chapter Fifteen

31

EVERYONE STILL BELIEVED that they had to continue doing as much as possible to coax Archie back to the age he had been when he checked himself into the hospital. When Yasuhiro refused to be born by dusk that evening, however, when he remained as firmly snuggled inside Ruby as he'd been on the day of his conception, they brought Archie down to walk around the block a couple of times, thinking that if that worked well, they might send him trick-or-treating with Gerard, as if he truly were just ten years old.

Who's bright idea was it? No one could remember when they asked themselves that question later on.

Bette brought three chairs out onto Ruby's stoop while Mr. Utterson and Ruby's father walked Archie twice around the block, as in a kind of test run. Gerard, whose excitement would *not* let him sit down, stood on the sidewalk in his freshly cleaned Mark Twain suit, Francesca beside him on her leash and wearing reindeer antlers. He was as happy as he had been on the day he got Francesca, and opened his umbrella when it started to rain again, so he wouldn't get his white wig wet. The other three men had passed by once already, arm in arm in arm.

"I'm going to knock on people's doors, and when they answer, I'll say 'Trick or treat!' to let them know what day it is!" Gerard said. "Maybe they forgot because they canceled the parade."

"Let's just hope it doesn't send them running for their shotguns. Halloween or not, can you imagine finding a Down syndrome man in a Colonel Sanders suit at your door, with a young Boo Radley beside him?" asked Bette.

"His name's not Boo; it's Archie!" Gerald said. "And I'm not supposed to be Colonel Sanders. You know that, Bette!"

Bette smiled down at him, pointed to the chair beside her, then reached over to wipe the raindrops off of it to make it more enticing to him. "Come on, honey, sit a minute," she said. "I know who you're supposed to be, I was just playing around."

Though he still didn't want to sit down, Gerard climbed slowly up the steps, dragging Francesca behind him. She wrinkled her face and stopped one step below him, pulling against her leash as hard as she could.

"I can't sit down because I'm going with them the next time around," Gerard explained, "We'll be trick-or-treating at our house, too, you know, so don't make yourselves too comfortable!"

"I haven't been comfortable in months," said Ruby, patting what she thought of as the top of Yasuhiro's head.

"Just remember to say 'Trick or treat' quietly when people answer their doors, Gerard," Bette said. "You'll scare the living shit out of everyone if you shout it."

But when they saw the men again, coming up the street to their right, Gerard shouted anyway. "Hi, Mr. Utterson! Hi, Ruby's father! Hi there, Archie Billingsly!" He then told the two women, "Look how wet they are! I better go meet them with my umbrella!"

Francesca had been trying to free herself on the step below him all this time, and when he turned and put his foot directly down on her, she let out a harrowing squeal. He lifted his foot again right away, but that only caused his other foot to lose its purchase on the step above. Ruby and Bette both reached out to steady him, Ruby missing him completely, and Bette managing only to pinch the sleeves of his Mark Twain suit before he started backstroking through the air, saying, "Whoa! Whoa! Whoa!"

Out of the corner of her eye, Ruby saw Mr. Utterson hurrying toward them, as if to try to stop Gerard's fall, but he was absurdly far away and Gerard was doing a pretty good job of stopping his fall by himself. His fat, square body and his wide, flat face, plus his stubby pumping arms, all served to give the impression of a giant flying squirrel trying to stay in its tree after losing its nerve for its first solo flight. He hooked his heels on the step above, rocking back and forth in the slowest of motions, until, as if the squirrel suddenly got its nerve back, he glided out over the cowering dog, then crashed down at normal speed, smashing into the bottommost step and bouncing along the sidewalk toward Mr. Utterson.

His umbrella pitched off toward Archie and Ruby's father, who caught it and brought it back and held it above him.

"Call 911," said Bette, and Ruby called them.

Gerard's eyes were open, but blood came from beneath both his ears and spread out, further darkening the already-wet sidewalk.

Everyone got to him quickly, even Ruby. Francesca was the last to arrive, and when she climbed onto his heaving chest, it brought such a powerful scream from Mr. Utterson that the neighbors across the street came outside, the girl and several of her friends in their Halloween costumes.

"What happened? What happened?" they called.

Mr. Utterson rolled up his jacket and laid it beneath Gerard's head, while the woman from across the street brought a blanket, her daughter took Francesca in her arms, and Bette administered CPR. It seemed to Ruby like a scene from one of her father's earliest paintings.

"May the Lord who frees you from sin save you and raise you up," said another of those who had gathered. It was Mary Andrew Michaelsonsen, come out from the nearby bushes, where she'd been hiding.

When Gerard tried to speak, Mr. Utterson put an ear against his lips lest his voice be weak, but it was strong. "You have reached the offices of Dr. Ruby G. Okada," he said. "We can't take your call right now, but please leave a message after the beep."

The ambulances arrived not ten minutes later, two of them coming from opposite ends of Bank Street.

That's when Ruby noticed that both Mary Andrew Michaelsonsen and Archie B. Billingsly were gone.

PART

THREE

Chapter Sixteen

32

Mr. Utterson slept in the parlor on Ruby's father's couch, while Bette sat stoically at the piano. Ruby herself had been up and down the stairs a half dozen times, when she should have been resting, for she couldn't help thinking that Archie might sneak back in to sit beside his train track, or even return as one of Bob's more bloodthirsty characters, to rain displeasure down on them all.

A phrase kept running through her head—*the best laid plans of mice and men*—though no one would accuse them of having well-laid plans. Their plans had been disastrous, weakly conceived, poorly executed, and most of them had been devised by her.

"Listen," she said, gently shaking Mr. Utterson, "I have to do my breathing exercises. Yasuhiro is three days late now, and my doctor says I'm not supposed to miss a single one of them. Why don't you do them with me, Gabriel, and then we'll both get a good night's sleep."

"That's my signal to go home," said Bette. "Good night, Rubescence. I won't be here tomorrow, but call me when your labor starts."

Ruby walked Bette outside. Mr. Utterson hadn't moved. He didn't seem to be thinking about her breathing exercises.

Ruby took Bette's arm but also held the railing as they stepped down to the street. For two days after Gerard's accident, they hadn't used the front door, but had circled down through the clinic and gone out that way. Now, however, they simply stepped where he had fallen, since the rain had washed all evidence of the blood away. Her father was outside, too, walking around the block with his head down, thinking whatever he thought. They could just see him now, turning the corner to their left.

"I had confidence that we could fix him. He was as sick as a man could be, but I still thought we could do it," Ruby said. "And now I don't even have the energy to look for him."

Bette struggled into her raincoat on the sidewalk.

"Not being able to fix someone is an occupational hazard for people like us," she said, "but energy to go out looking for him? What are you, kidding? You're as pregnant as a harvest moon. Let me worry about Archie, let Mr. Utterson worry about Gerard, and ask your father to do your breathing exercises with you. That's why he's here, in case you've forgotten."

Bette had ridden her bicycle over the night before. She hadn't pulled it into Ruby's foyer nor chained it to a lamppost, but it stood where she'd left it, red and wet and waiting. She brushed the water off its saddle, swung her right leg up over it, and settled down. The lady from across the street was on her stoop with her daughter and waved to them.

"Don't you dare not call me," said Bette. "I want to be there when *that* little trick-or-treater comes knocking, no matter how long it takes."

She pushed away from the curb and rode off toward West Fourth Street.

Now that Ruby was outside, she didn't want to go back in. She wanted a bike of her own to sail around the block on. She imagined the smoothness of its ride, the coasting around potholes, the swerving to miss pedestrians. In yet another dream she'd had the night after Gerard got hurt, Bob came to kneel beside her bed and whisper to her. She'd been able to see both him and herself in the dream, plus Gerard sitting in her father's room, writing a letter to Hal Holbrook. It was then that *the best laid plans of mice and men* came to her, and when she said it aloud, Bob spoke.

"In the original poem it's 'schemes,'" he had said. "'The best laid schemes o' Mice an' Men / Gang aft agley, / An' lea'e us nought but grief an' pain / For promis'd joy!'"

He said that *gang aft agley* meant "often go wrong," before standing and leaving again.

Though she'd had more than her fill of dreams, when she woke the following morning, she went to look through that telescope, as if Bob had told her to. Guido slept beside it on the ottoman.

"The last time I actually used this thing, I saw Archie on the picnic table, but now I see only the shambles of my life," she told her cat, before spotting Francesca down in the backyard, Mr. Utterson beside her, protective and gentle and worried and heartbroken. Francesca had also disappeared when Gerard got hurt, but here she was again, those reindeer antlers still somehow clinging to her head.

As Ruby hurried down to help Mr. Utterson, she had the thought that none of the important moments of her recent life, from her move to this house through Mary Andrew

Michaelsonsen's visit, from finding a wounded Archie in her yard through her father's arrival and this grievous injury to Gerard . . . none of these moments were catalysts for her, because there were no catalysts in life. Life simply and only went on until it stopped.

By the time she got to Mr. Utterson that morning, he was standing with Francesca in his arms. "Did I ever tell you how I first met Gerard?" he asked. "I'd been given tickets to *Mark Twain Tonight* by one of my clients. I used to love the theater but hadn't been in years, and I didn't intend to go then, either, until something made me leave my lonely dinner and drive in to see it in my taxi. This was midtown Manhattan on a weekend night, I am talking about, so even the parking garages were full. I circled the streets in dead-slow traffic, about to shake myself loose from a bad idea and go back home again, when Gerard appeared, smiling like the sun had just come out, to guide me into a newly vacated parking spot. When I got out of my car and tried to tip him, he said, 'Guess who's here tonight! It's Hal Holbrook! I'm Gerard Holbrook. Gerard isn't short for anything, but Hal is short for Harold!'

"When I said I had tickets to the show, and gave him my extra one . . . well, that made us friends for life."

Extra tickets seemed to be a theme in the lives of people Ruby loved.

Mr. Utterson had told that story on November 1, and now, two days later, Ruby waited for her father to come around the block again, and when she took him back inside, Mr. Utterson was in the kitchen, cooking bacon and eggs.

"Gerard used to love it when I made him breakfast for dinner," he said. "He liked his eggs over easy. Once, he even tried to pack his Tupperware with them, but they ran through its seams. How about you? Are you an over-easy woman, Ruby? And how do you like your eggs, Mr. Okada? I'm an over-well man, myself. I hope that doesn't make me Orwellian?"

He'd tried several times to be lighthearted since Gerard's accident, always unsuccessfully. Such jokes only made him seem pitiful.

"Orwellian for me, too, but just one egg," said Ruby's father.

When Ruby said she'd take hers the way Gerard liked his, and then asked Mr. Utterson if he knew the meaning of *gang aft agley,* he said, "If memory serves, it means 'keep the ugly ones behind you.' It was a rule of thumb when I was growing up, for the ugly ones were often the bullies."

Was there something wrong with a lightness of spirit when they didn't know if Gerard would live or die? Part of her said there was, and part of her said there was not.

"I've been telling Yasuhiro that he mustn't be born until Gerard gets well," said Ruby. "Do you think that's too tall an order? He's three days late as it is, my baby."

Mr. Utterson brought their eggs to the table, garnished with parsley and a quarter section of an orange. He put his egg atop a slice of buttered toast, then used his fork to smash it down and spread it out.

When he stood again to get the bacon he'd forgotten, the strips of which were latticed on their plate, Ruby thought of the light that had latticed the hallway floor on the morning Gerard first arrived in his Mark Twain suit. When she said as much, a tear ran down the cracked-egg surface of Mr. Utterson's face.

She saw the shadow of her father's hand as it hovered over the bacon, as he stopped to watch the tear's descent.

33

AFTER RUBY DID HER BREATHING EXERCISES, and when her father went up to his room for a moment, she found an old umbrella and stepped outside again.

The sidewalk was empty now, giving her plenty of opportunity to look before each step in order to avoid the pavement separations that might send her sprawling. Soon, however, she found herself avoiding pavement cracks as well as separations, placing her feet down only on unblemished surfaces, just as she had as a child. She didn't want to break her mother's back on the eve of her own motherhood.

She wore her dad's old nylon Mariners jacket, and as she tried to watch her feet, she remembered a particular elementary school day when she was something like nine years old. Nothing had happened at school that day, nor on her way home, but at a corner where she stood alone in a yellow rain slicker, she had the thought that she was pinned down upon the earth, and that the earth was spinning in an incomprehensible vastness. That was all, yet she remembered that moment often, perhaps too pleased with having had such a thought at such a young age. . . . And she remembered it now because of her earlier thought that there were no catalysts in life. Pinned down without catalysts in an incomprehensible vastness . . . That was something she would share with Mr. Utterson the next time he felt the need to have a cheerful talk.

At Ninth Avenue, she waited for the light.

She wasn't alone on the sidewalk anymore; others swarmed around her in her slowness, holding hands or walking arm in arm. They formed geometric shapes that split when they got to her, then joined again on her other side, as if she were a breakwater . . . as if she were a river boulder or a rock that held a lighthouse eleven miles out.

A clock in the window of a shop on the other side of Ninth Avenue said 8:30, but another beside it said 1:15, and clocks both higher and lower insisted on 7:11 and 3:45. Four clocks in a clock shop with four different times.

"If I owned this place, I would never let that happen," said a man who'd stopped beside her. "What confidence would it give you that the clock you buy here would keep good time?"

Ruby put her hands down below her bulging abdomen, fingers spread wide. She turned to face her father, who had followed her. "I'm thinking of going back to the hospital," she said. "I'd like to visit Gerard just once without having to look at Mr. Utterson's worried face."

When her father asked if she wanted to go without him, too, and she said that she did not, he flagged a taxi and told the driver, "Roosevelt Hospital, over on Tenth Avenue at Fifty-ninth."

The driver was young and Indian or Pakistani, dressed in a hoodie, with the hood pushed back off his head. He sat on a beaded seat cover and had a book beside him. What if he spent the endless hours of his night shift memorizing lines, or reenacting events in India or Pakistan?

It was only when they got to the hospital and were lifted slowly in an ancient elevator that her father wondered if there were stricter rules for visiting hours in the ICU than in the rest of the hospital, like there were in Japan. He had been in America for more than forty years, and still he had to ask such things.

Ruby had no idea what the answer was, but at the nurses' station, when they saw a friendly day-shift nurse and Ruby said, "Hi, remember us?" the nurse only smiled and told them, "He's in room six now. We'll miss your visits when your baby comes. Do you know if it's a boy or girl?"

Ruby nearly said "I know it's Yasuhiro," but when the nurse looked back at her paperwork, she kept her mouth shut, and avoided the cracks in the linoleum as they made their way down the hall.

Room six had no lock on its door. Not even a doorknob. Not even a doorknob hole to stick a screwdriver in and lever up and back. Rather, it had a long brass plate, which her father put his hands on and shoved, a long brass plate with the germs of other sets of hands still alive upon it.

Room six was plainer than the room Gerard had been in before, which had been number thirty-six, if she remembered correctly, thirty rooms higher on the hopeful scale. There were four metal chairs around the edge of the room, all of which looked smudged. Ruby's father brought two of them close to the gurney that held Gerard, who was covered by a crisp starched sheet and blanket, folded and tucked up tightly around his shoulders. His eyes were closed, but his mouth was open, and drool ran in rivulets down his chin. Ruby found some tissue and dried up all the rivulets, and tried several times to close his mouth. His skin was the color of parchment and his hair, though combed, wasn't combed correctly. Someone had tried to work around the gash in his head by giving him an old man's comb-over. She hadn't understood why she'd had the urge to come here again so late, but this was why. Whatever happened later, Gerard had to look right. Beside him stood the various monitors and tubes that were necessary to keep him alive.

"Do you have a comb, Dad?" she asked. "And do you happen to have any gel?"

When her father buzzed a hand across the top of his head, she pulled Gerard's sheet and blanket back until his naked upper chest came out of it. His flesh looked soft and was the color of a cloud with the sun lit up behind it. A table next to him held a metal surgical tray with Ziploc plastic bags. One contained his stud earring, the other a partial bridge with two molars. When Ruby said, "I didn't know he had false teeth," her father said, "How about we put his earring back?"

Without waiting for her response, he opened the earring bag, took out the stud, and slipped it through Gerard's big earlobe. When Ruby found the nerve to touch his ear the way her father had, she found that it was malleable.

"We're never going to make his hair look good if we don't have any gel," she said.

She opened the drawer of a nearby table, which held only a box of latex gloves and some Q-tips and cotton swabs. Anyone could die in this room; here, Gerard was equal to everyone else.

When she pushed on the swinging door again and stepped back out into the hall, her father stayed where he was. She saw that the wing they had moved Gerard to had small stands in front of most of its rooms, with the names of patients stuck into metal slots at their tops. She'd somehow missed that when they went in, but of course it reminded her of Boys of Summer, when she first saw Henry Hyde. Those rooms held people down on their luck, while these held people whose luck had run out. Carmen Esposito was across the hall from Gerard, and one door down was Frank Collins. She didn't want to enter anyone else's room, but what if they had gel?

When she pushed Frank Collins's door open, she saw an old man wheezing on his bed, his body emaciated and a low death rattle churning away in his throat. He had sores on the parts of his body that were exposed, but his eyes darted over to her when he heard her come in. A worried bird, she thought.

"Mr. Collins, how did things come to this?" she asked.

It was what she always asked herself, so why not ask him?

On a table exactly like the one in Gerard's room stood a jar of Vaseline, so she opened it and scooped some onto her fingers and applied it to Mr. Collins's sores, until he closed his terrible eyes and his death rattle grew faint. His Adam's apple protruded like a snowcapped mountain from a plain. She scooped more Vaseline onto her palm and closed the jar again.

In the hallway, she held her right hand out, cupped as if the Vaseline were liquid and might spill onto the floor. Frank Collins, Carmen Esposito, Gerard Holbrook . . . From Boys of Summer she remembered Mr. Lamb and Mr. Poole and Mrs. Florentino. She pushed Gerard's door back open with her shoulder and went directly to him. Her father sat in one of those straight-backed chairs.

"I brought too much of this," she said, and it was true. When she held out her hand, she imagined a pitched and murky sea, or a mountain range immersed in fog. . . . She could see Mr. Collins's Adam's apple as clearly as if she'd brought it along.

"Too much is better than not enough," her father said.

She turned her hand over and brushed the Vaseline across the top of Gerard's head, until his hair stood up in a good imitation of how he liked to wear it—cool, but not too cool, a workingman's hip. She used her other hand to pull his sheet and blanket back into place, her gooey fingers now at her side.

She felt that their time alone with Gerard should include

more than just this busyness, that it ought to contain a prayer or meditation, something to let him know that they would never give up on him, though it seemed clear that the hospital might have. But when no prayer or meditation came to her, she said, "Okay, Gerard, we're going now, but we'll be back in the morning if my baby's not born."

Without remembering not to do so, she raised her gelled hand up and saluted him.

It left a Vaseline smear on her forehead, an inch or so above her right eye.

Chapter Seventeen

34

T HE NEXT DAY, SUNDAY, NOVEMBER 4, Mr. Utterson went to the hospital without them, taking food from Gerard's favorite deli, either to lay before him like Hindus lay food before gods or eat himself while sitting in one of those uncomfortable chairs. He wanted to take Francesca with him, but when Ruby said that dogs weren't allowed in the hospital, he left her with Ruby and her father, who were once more eating eggs in the kitchen.

"Do you know the word *closure,* Dad, which has become so popular lately?" Ruby asked when she was sure that Mr. Utterson was gone. "I think it means putting uncomfortable things behind you."

"I know that it's a fraudulent word and stands in front of a fraudulent concept," he said. "It wants to make things neat, like closing a door."

Ruby believed that, too, but she wanted to talk about closure for a little while anyway, fraudulent concept or not, And she would have had her father not said, "I'd like to get busy on the tree house this morning. Do you want to come help?"

He used his fork to gesture out the window at the tree house tree, detritus surrounding it again after the storm.

"I can sit out there with you, but I don't know about helping," she said, "except for maybe handing you your tools. Do you know where I think I might start to feel a little bit of closure, Dad? It's with Yasuhiro. Although I think he's decided to stay where he is, to cut his loses by simply not being born." She paused, then added, "How about we take Mom's mask outside and nail it to the tree house tree, too. That might bring me another kind of closure. You don't mind if the mask gets battered after this, by the changing seasons of your grandson's life?"

Here they were again, just as they had been during vast stretches of her earlier life, her father's urge to get things done trumping her urge to talk to him.

"We could hang it under the rope ladder," he said. "That way, whenever Yasuhiro climbs it, he can watch his grandmother's altering age."

That made Ruby love her father dearly. The face of her son flashed by for a second, also, but far too quickly for her to notice.

Almost as soon as he started work, her father's trips up and down the backyard staircase drew Francesca and Guido outside, she to lie on shifting patches of sunlight, he to sit atop the stack of wood that had been delivered two days earlier, when all of them were at the hospital.

Ruby brought a blanket to sit on, a thermos of water, her mother's mask, and, almost as an afterthought, Archie O. Billingsly's scrapbook. This was the Archie born the same year as her father, and dead at thirty-six.

"We got swept up with Archie S. Billingsly before," she said, "so I thought I'd try this guy now."

"Like me, he never knew his father. But unlike me, he also didn't get to know his child," her father said.

She liked that. It sounded to her like a compliment.

The shifting patches of sunlight, the first since the storm, made Francesca stand and move occasionally, and turn in little circles and sit back down. Ruby, too, moved and felt calm. Maybe there wasn't any closure, but they were building a tree house for her son.

"I think it will need two rooms," she said. "The front one big enough for him to share with friends, the back one meant for him to sleep in by himself."

"Or with his mother," said her father. "Like your mother used to sleep outside with you."

"Mom didn't sleep outside with me, Dad. That was you. In fact, I can only remember her visiting my tree house once or twice."

She remembered that pall, and picked up the mask to try to find it on its forehead. But Bette was right: The skin on her mother's Noh mask face was flawless.

"What are you talking about, sweetheart? She slept in your tree house often," said her father, "sometimes for days at a time. It was me who slept there less, for I didn't like the damp night air."

Though she knew as well as anyone that memories could be false, it couldn't be true, what her father'd said now. Her mother had been distant, her father distant but close. Instead of saying no again, however, she struggled to her feet with the mask.

"Let's nail this up there now," she said. "Whatever her habits were before, she can be a talisman, maybe even a good-luck charm."

"A good-luck charm is what she always was," he said. "In Kyoto, when I carved her, I was down on my luck, couldn't sell a painting, couldn't find my life. But after I carved her, things turned around."

Ruby stood again and stepped past the stack of lumber, put her mother's mask up against the tree trunk. She asked, "How did she change your luck?" She moved the mask to her face and looked at her father through its eyes. *"You didn't meet me until you saw me in the park,"* she made it say. *"And followed me to my tavern."*

She could tell he didn't like her doing that again, but when she put the mask back down, he came over with a couple of boards he'd cut, hammered one of them into the tree to make a shelf, checked the shelf with his level, then picked up three more boards and in no time turned the shelf into a box. When Ruby put the mask inside it, it looked as if her mother had heard a knock from inside her tree home and come to open a door within the door in order to see who was there.

"Avon lady," Ruby told her mother's face.

She turned to her father, who was smiling ruefully now, as if telling her that they shouldn't be traveling so far afield of the issues of the last three days: Gerard's grave condition, Archie's disappearance, Yasuhiro's refusal to be born.

She put the mask against the tree again. "So after you carved her, your luck changed right away?" she asked. "How'd that happen, Dad?"

"I was repairing a house I had rented in Kyoto, and the owner often came to see what improvements I had made. He especially liked my rotten straw wall—*kyo-kabe*, we used to call it. My paintings were around, some of them hanging, some on the floor, and one day my Jittoku pals were sitting beside the paintings, drinking whiskey, when the owner walked in with his father. Some of my friends were foreigners."

Ruby sat down on her blanket again, pulled Archie O. Billingsly's scrapbook onto her lap, and opened it. He had lived from 1944 to 1980, and the year her father spoke of now was 1972 or '73.

"One of my American friends took pride in his fluent Japanese and began to pretend that he had come to buy the painting that happened to be beside him—an unfinished piece depicting two men sitting in a forest—which I had started calling *Otoko wa Damatte,* which means something like 'men not talking.'"

Ruby could see her father's painting in her mind's eye, but the eyes in her head fell down upon a photograph of Archie O. Billingsly, sitting in a bar and holding up a glass of whiskey, much like one of her father's Kyoto friends might have done. Someone had written below the picture "Our own Archie, celebrating." *Our own Archie . . .* Was that not an expression of love?

"The landlord had brought his father from a village outside Kyoto in order to show off my *kyo-kabe* walls," her father said. "His father, like mine, had fought in the war. He didn't like foreigners, and when he heard my bar friend pretend to offer a very high price for my painting, he said, '*Otoko wa Damatte* must remain in Japan,' and offered twice as much himself."

"So your friend was a shill," said Ruby. "Your luck didn't change because of the mask, but because the wounds of war had not yet healed."

She looked at Archie O. Billingsly's photo again. "If your father had lived, he would have hated my father's father," she told it.

"But it *was* the mask that changed my luck," said her father, "for the mask was in the room that day, too, leaning against a pillar and looking at *Otoko wa Damatte* like an art critic. My landlord's father raised the price again but said he wanted the mask, as well."

Ruby turned the scrapbook's page, but the rest of the scrapbook was empty.

"Well, you obviously didn't sell him the mask," she said. "For here it is now, sitting in a box on our tree house tree. So how did it change your luck?"

Just as she was about to thumb through the scrapbook from its beginning, something flittered out of it on a sudden puff of breeze, landing next to Guido, who promptly put his paw on it. It wasn't a letter this time, but a one-by-three-inch newspaper clipping.

"My friends thought it would be a great idea to get rid of a failed Noh mask and receive three hundred and fifty thousand yen—nearly one thousand dollars at the time—for the painting, but when I saw the look on the Noh mask's face, its truly negative opinion of *Otoko wa Damatte*, I suddenly realized how sentimental the painting was, how derivative in its abstract aspect of Picasso and his cohorts. The Noh mask was right—the painting was bad—so I kicked the landlord and his father out, burned the painting a few days later, and, with your mother's Noh mask as my guide, began to make something like actual art."

Ruby had her eyes on that newspaper clipping, its headline barely visible to her below the furry mound of Guido's paw: LOCAL ARTIST HANGS HIMSELF.

"You mean after that you looked to the mask's expression to tell you whether something you made was good or bad, and then came to America and found Mom?" she asked. "I don't know, Dad, that sounds a little too freaky, even for you."

"It was freakier than freaky, but I didn't ask the mask's opinion. After that, I simply worked as hard as I could."

35

LOCAL ARTIST HANGS HIMSELF

New York claymation artist Archie O. Billingsly was found on Sunday last, hanging from a tree in the backyard of his West Village home. Mr. Billingsly's short claymation film, *Pieces of Eight,* won him early recognition. Based on the Robert Louis Stevenson classic, *Treasure Island,* the film featured Long John Silver's parrot, Captain Flint. Mr. Billingsly is survived by his grandmother, Anna Stevenson Billingsly, and by a four-year-old son, Archie B. Billingsly.

The family has announced that services will be private.

Ruby read the clipping while resting in her bedroom a few hours later, her father's constant hammer blows echoing in from outside. It was a sound she knew from childhood, and one that made her calm. What she *hadn't* known from childhood, hadn't known till now, was that claymation even existed back in 1980. She had snooped around the house when she came inside, hoping to find a VHS, or even an old eight-millimeter movie reel of *Pieces of Eight*, but found nothing more belonging to Archie O. Billingsly. It was as if his grandmother had erased any sign of him at the time of his death. Except for that photo in the stairwell.

She put the newspaper clipping inside the copy of *Dr. Jekyll and Mr. Hyde* that still lay on her bedside table, and shifted around on her bed in a futile attempt to make herself more comfortable.

"Come help me solve all these mysteries, Yasuhiro," she said; "your stake in it is bigger than mine. Surely he didn't hang himself from your tree house tree. You don't think so, do you?"

Bang, bang, bang, her father's hammer kept saying.

What was the word for Yasuhiro's decision to stay put? It surely wasn't *closure*. It was closure's opposite. Would *hiatus* do, or *sequestered*? Was he refusing to move from that world to this one because the jury was still out on the fate of his father?

She got up and went into the hallway and climbed the stairs to Archie's room, where his train still stood, its passengers still lined up, the conductor still looking at his watch. She sat down cross-legged by the train's controls, and when she turned on the power, she was sure she saw the briefest puff of pure white smoke curl up from the engine's smokestack.

"What are they doing," she asked the conductor, "electing a new Pope?"

When she pushed the control lever forward, the train started to move, and when she pulled the lever back, it stopped.

"Cool," she said. "I could get into this. Do you want to get into it with me, Yasuhiro? We can both wear one of these caps."

She picked up the cap that Gerard had worn, that grandfather's clock song tick-tocking in her head. It was a song that made a person's life seem long, when really a life passed in the blink of an eye; everyone knew that.

Blink, gone.

Chapter Eighteen

36

THREE MORE DAYS PASSED before Gerard began to show signs of emerging from his coma. During those days, Ruby's father finished the tree house, with Ruby often walking around its base, chatting with him and also trying to decide if it could be the tree from which Archie O. Billingsly had hanged himself. Could she let her son climb the ladder that her father was just now finishing if it led to the branch from which his paternal grandfather had swayed?

In every way but one, the week following Gerard's accident seemed calmer than those preceding it. Mr. Utterson, ubiquitous at Ruby's house before the accident, now spent his days sitting beside Gerard; and, in order to catch up at work, Bette started doing double shifts at the hospital. So Ruby and her father had the house to themselves and lived the life they knew how to live with each other. They took walks, did Ruby's breathing exercises, and looked out the back door at Ruby's mother's mask, still in that box on the tree.

The one way in which things were not calmer after Gerard's accident had to do with Yasuhiro's radical decrease in movement. For a while, Ruby didn't inform her OB-GYN, but now, on day seven after his due date, she was on her way to an appointment with Dr. Muir, when Mr. Utterson called with news that Gerard had opened his eyes and had asked if Francesca was mad at him for stepping on her.

"We'll get there as soon as we can," Ruby told him. "I just want to swing by Dr. Muir's office first."

She and her father were in the living room, their coats over their arms.

"Should I call Bette?" Mr. Utterson asked. "Would she come, too, if I asked her?"

Ah those breasts! Ruby thought.

But to be at the end of things freed Mr. Utterson, and it freed Ruby, too. When she hung up, she took her father's arm and looked out the window at the house across the street. The girl stood at the bottom of her stoop in a party dress. Through the open door above the girl, Ruby could see balloons. Perhaps it was her birthday and she was waiting for her guests. Ruby liked that girl, remembered how bravely she had lifted Francesca from Gerard's chest. She didn't think the girl could see her, but when she waved, the girl waved back, then shrugged, as if to say, Everyone's late!

Ruby put a finger up, gave her father her coat, and went to the bookshelves to pull down a copy of *Treasure Island*. There were a dozen copies of it, plus a dozen more of *Dr. Jekyll and Mr. Hyde*, but all Bob's other titles, even *Kidnapped*, had long ago vanished from the house.

A few old bookmarks were scattered on the bookshelves, one with an image of Bell Rock Lighthouse on it. When she opened *Treasure Island* to place that bookmark inside, she saw the inscription *"to a very fine, very good child,"* with no capital letter at its beginning. The writing was spindly and was clearly in a woman's hand, probably that of Archie's tormentor. Had she meant to give it to Archie on his birthday but had not because his recitation was flawed?

Ruby put that volume back and picked up another, this one with no inscription. Before she and her father stepped outside, she slid the book beneath her shirt, where it rested on top of the slumbering Yasuhiro. They had just gotten to the bottom of their steps when the girl's mother appeared in the doorway across the street to call, "Adriana! sweetheart, don't go too far."

Sweetheart . . . what her father had recently called her.

A car swung onto Bank Street and stopped to deposit three more girls, all bearing gifts and wearing party dresses. Ruby squeezed her father's arm.

The woman delivering the new girls spoke to Adriana's mother for a minute, both of them laughing and nodding, and when she pulled out again, a one-legged man stood not ten feet from Adriana, leaning against a single crutch. A one-legged man whom Ruby knew well.

"I'm walking here!" he shouted. "Don't clutter the street with little wenches!"

At first, Ruby thought his leg was actually missing, but then she saw that it was tied up behind him by an odd combination of belts and ropes. It was as clearly rigged a costume as Gerard's (or Hal Holbrook's) Mark Twain . . . as clearly a reenactment as any her father's four Scotsmen might have devised.

Adriana's mother froze, all the girls shrieked, and the other woman stopped her car again in the middle of the street, turned off its engine, and got out.

"Did you just call them 'wenches'?" she said. "Listen here, buddy, tell me I heard you wrong!"

"Of course they're wenches!" croaked Long John Silver. "Like them women that stroll Bristol Harbor when the ships come in, hoping to slip their hands into a randy sailor's pocket."

He pulled out one of his own pockets, letting it fall down like a tongue.

"Is he some sort of party clown?" the driver asked Adriana's mom.

"That's exactly what he is," said Ruby, "but he's got the house wrong! And it's not a party; it's a vigil for our injured friend, who so loves pirates that we thought we might take one to the hospital with us."

She hurried across to the street to stand by Long John Silver.

"No need to start acting yet," she told him. "We won't head over to the hospital for another half hour or so."

"He doesn't even really have a missing leg. It's right there behind him, where everyone can see. It's not even scary that way," said Adriana.

When she pointed at his tied-up leg, she took a tentative step toward him.

"I'll have you know I lost me leg, fighting under Edward Hawke at the second battle of Finisterre!" Long John Silver said. "If you start spouting lies, little lassie, yer mother will have to wash yer mouth out with bilge soap."

"Good grief, bilge soap?" said Adriana's mother, laughing a little bit now.

"Use a soap of yer liking," said the pirate, "but a bilge soap washing is a memorable experience."

"He's a family friend, and literary figures are his specialty," Ruby's father said. "You should hear him do Mishima, shouting his right-wing speech from the self-defense force's balcony. He's entirely convincing."

He went to the pirate and reached down to grab a loose

strand of rope, releasing all the knots and ties in one lucky pull. The leg came down like something hydraulic. When it touched the sidewalk, the girls all laughed, as did the departing mother.

"Literary figures, eh?" she said. "Come on, then, give us a taste of someone else before I go."

"Yes, be someone else! Be someone who tells a story!" said Adriana.

Ruby felt him use both legs to steady himself, then saw him doff an invisible hat, much like Dr. Livesey had done. He twisted the hat before him and said in a boy's clear voice, *"Sometimes the isle was thick with savages, with whom we fought; sometimes full of dangerous animals that hunted us; but in all my fancies nothing occurred to me so strange and tragic as our actual adventures."*

"What adventures? What adventures!" asked all four girls.

When they skipped over to stand in front of him, he bent to look into each set of eyes.

"You know that pirate who was just here?" he asked conspiratorially. "Well, his stories frighten people most. Dreadful stories they are about hangings and walking the plank, about storms at sea and the Dry Tortugas, and wild deeds and places on the Spanish Main. By his own account, he lived his life among the wickedest men the sea ever belched out, and the language he uses to tell their stories shocks our plain country people almost as much as the crimes he describes."

"Oh, oh, oh!" said each new girl, while Adriana said, "Oh Mom, thank you! This is the best party ever! I like stories about wicked people, and since today's my birthday, I want one."

"Then one is what you'll get," said Young Jim Hawkins. *"I remember him as if it were yesterday, as he came plodding to the inn door, his sea-chest following behind him in a hand-barrow, a tall, strong, heavy, nut-brown man; his tarry pigtail falling over the shoulder of his soiled blue coat; his hands ragged and scarred, with black, broken nails; and the saber cut across one cheek, a dirty, livid white. I remember him looking round the cover and whistling to himself as he did so, and then breaking out in that old sea-song that he sang so often afterwards: 'Fifteen men on the dead man's chest—Yo-ho-ho and a bottle of rum!'"*

"Okay, stop." Adriana's mother laughed. "Don't get me wrong, I believe you could make a living doing this, but I've got pizza and cannolis, and a piñata hanging from a tree in our backyard."

"In the immediate nearness of the gold, all else had been forgotten; . . . and I could not doubt that he hoped to seize upon the treasure, find and board the Hispaniola *under cover of night, cut every honest throat about that island, and sail away as he had at first intended, laden with crimes and riches."*

"You girls go cut the throat of that piñata," said Adriana's mother. "If we hear any more of this, none of us will sleep tonight."

To Ruby's surprise, the girls did as they were told, either because they were sufficiently frightened by then or because they wanted a taste of the piñata's blood.

Until then, she'd forgotten the book she'd brought, but now slipped it from its hiding place and lifted it up so its jacket faced Adriana, who had turned and come back. It showed two pirates in the foreground, one with a pistol in each hand and the other carrying a cutlass. Behind them, another pirate hoisted the Jolly Roger from a pitching ship's deck.

"My gosh, was this all a prelude to giving her that book!"

asked Adriana's mother. "What an extraordinary gift! Adriana, look!"

"Hey! That's my 1911 first edition!" said Archie. "It's worth a hundred bucks at least."

"It's a birthday gift and also a thank-you for helping us the other day, coming to the aid of our dear friend," Ruby said.

Adriana took the book and curtsied. When she said "I will keep it as a treasure by my bed!" the power of her earnestness seemed to drive Archie inward again, and bring Bob out to watch the exchange. It was the last thing Ruby wanted in the world, but there he was.

"It's a beautiful edition! I'm delighted to see it, delighted to know that it's still read!" he said. "I wrote that book when pretending to be Captain George North, you know. Would you like me to sign it for you?"

At first, Ruby saw that this was the last thing Adriana wanted—some bad actor signing her book—but the searching aspect of his far-apart eyes made her say in a moment, "Mommy, do you have your pen? Sign your name and say something nice to me. And use good penmanship, okay?"

"I will use the penmanship of kings," Bob said. "But let me see, then . . . oh yes! How's this?"

He opened the book to its title page and wrote out carefully, "to a very fine, very good child." And then he wrote below it, quickly and with a flourish, *Robert Louis Stevenson*, taking up the rest of the page.

PART
FOUR

Chapter Nineteen

37

GERARD'S HOMECOMING WAS NO SMALL THING. Mr. Utterson ran in and out of Ruby's basement several times, bringing the items that the people at the hospital had told him were necessary to assure Gerard's continued good care. Because his room was in a medical clinic, the hospital authorities had released him to Mr. Utterson—but also because Mr. Utterson had drawn up an ersatz power of attorney and presented it to them. He was not in the least a man inclined to Cain's heresy. "Not once did they ask if I was kin to him," he said. "Do you think that's because he has Down syndrome?"

"Well, he doesn't exactly *have* Down syndrome," said Bette. "It isn't something you catch."

Gerard was in bed, his eyes moving toward whoever spoke. "Francesca's mad, and Guido's mad, too," he said. "I count one mad cat and one mad dog."

Ruby stood behind the others, watching Gerard watch them. Dr. Muir had told her that Yasuhiro was simply strong-willed, that otherwise nothing was wrong. But Ruby always kept her hands beneath her abdomen now, as if that was where they belonged.

"They're not mad; they're outside watching the tree house go up," said Mr. Utterson, but Gerard's eyes had closed again.

"They said at the hospital that this would happen—one minute awake, thirty minutes sleeping," he said. "We're supposed to wake him if he tries to sleep longer than that."

Ruby remembered a lecture from medical school about not letting those with head injuries sleep for too long, but it also seemed like something Dr. Livesey might say, so perhaps it had once been true but wasn't anymore. She said she'd watch him first, let the others get about their business.

"Good. I need a shower and a change of clothes. I'll be back in an hour or two," said Bette.

"And I will go buy some treats for him," Mr. Utterson told her.

When they left, Ruby sat beside Gerard, noting from his bedside clock that it was 2:23. At 2:53, she would wake him. One minute awake to thirty minutes sleeping seemed a pretty good ratio to her, though a vastly more generous apportionment to waking than the ratio of time spent living against time spent dead.

"What do you think, Gerardino? Would you like to keep on slumbering or wake and check your e-mail, on the chance that Hal Holbrook is back from his tour?"

Gerard's eyes opened, but there wasn't any light in them. She used to catch dogfish with eyes like that, when fishing with her father on Puget Sound.

"Yasuhiro seems to be where you are now," she said. "How about telling him it's time to be born?"

She stifled the urge to close Gerard's eyes with her hand.

High up on the wall, a window looked out into her backyard. She'd peered through it from the other direction often, when outside watching her father work, when Gerard was in the hospital and she didn't think he would come home again. But he *had* come home, and now he was in the bed beside her with his dogfish eyes.

She stood and went to the window and looked out. From this perspective, she could see the base of Yasuhiro's tree but not the tree house itself. She did have an unobstructed view of her mother's mask, however, still staring out from the door within the door of the tree, as if watching the path in front of it. "Hi, Mom, it's me, come to visit and carrying your grandson," she said. "He's eight days late. Could you try to convince him to join the world?"

She turned back to Gerard, to whom she'd just made that same request, but his eyes had fallen closed again. His clock said 2:52. Had she been standing at that window for twenty-nine minutes? That seemed impossible, but there it was.

She stepped back over and gently shook his toe.

"I spy with my little eye . . ." he said, though his eyes remained shut.

"What do you spy?" she asked. "How do you play that game again? I forgot."

"You have to try to guess what I'm looking at. I'll give you a hint if you want one, but not until after you make a first guess."

"You're looking at the inside of your eyelids. They're black, with an aura of red."

She'd closed her own eyes so she could describe the scene correctly, and when she opened them again, Gerard's were open, too.

"Okay, then," she said. "Give me that hint."

"I did what you asked me to . . ."

"What's that, Gerard? I didn't ask you to do anything."

"No, Dr. Okada, 'I did what you asked me to . . .' *is* the hint."

She had asked him, of course, to nudge her stubborn son into life.

She was about to ask him for a different hint—that one was far too frightening—but his minute of wakefulness was up.

38

RUBY DIDN'T WANT TO TALK ABOUT yesterday's incident at Adriana's birthday party. When her father told Bette and Mr. Utterson what had happened, they'd asked her questions, of course, but she would only say that she didn't want to talk about it.

She couldn't avoid thinking about it, though, so while Gerard was sleeping, she went over everything one more time, by remembering those who'd appeared on the street and those who had not. Long John Silver and Young Jim Hawkins and Archie had all been there, and Bob with his book signing, but there'd been no sign of Mr. Hyde. Or Mary Andrew Michaelsonsen, either, so perhaps Archie had abandoned the most terrifying of his characters, and Mary Andrew had abandoned him. Perhaps he was alone now, fending for himself on some other nearby street.

She'd forgotten to note the beginning of Gerard's second sleep, so decided on 3:00 P.M. Asleep at 3:00, awake at 3:30, asleep at 3:31 . . .

She walked out of his room with his clock in her hands. Her clinic was bathed in the closed-down darkness that one most often associated with businesses that had already failed.

She could remember the day she'd opened the clinic, but from that day to this she hadn't had a single patient, if you didn't count Mary Andrew Michaelsonsen. . . . No one, not one.

When she saw the light blinking on her office telephone, she imagined that whoever left a message had heard Gerard say "We can't take your call right now" in his faux British accent, and she had the thought that those seven words could be the universal message of the living to the dead as they rolled through all the generations. *We can't take your call right now* . . . Except once, according to Bob in her dream.

She picked up the phone, stifling the urge to say hello.

"Ruby, it's me," said Bette. "Call me back the instant you get this!"

It hadn't been an hour since Bette left. The door to Gerard's room had been closed during that time, but even so she thought she'd have been able to hear the telephone ring. She picked it up and dialed Bette's number, which rang and rang and rang. She hung up and dialed again.

"Yeah?" Bette said.

"What do you mean 'Yeah'?" asked Ruby. "You called me."

"You know I can't do that. This is New York State," Bette said. "Why don't you move to Oregon? Maybe what you need to solve your problems is a change of scene."

"What?" Ruby asked, a second before she understood that Bette was talking to someone else.

She imagined Bette's phone hidden in her lap, or lying in an open drawer.

"Come over here and sit across from me," said Bette. "I don't like people standing in my doorway."

A few times before, men had come to the hospital demanding drugs, so they'd installed panic buttons in everyone's office.

Why hadn't Bette pushed that, then, instead of calling Ruby? Or why hadn't she dialed 911?

"You owe me," said the man.

Now that Ruby could hear him clearly, she sat down hard on the chair at Gerard's desk.

"I don't owe you fuck-all, but sit down anyway; maybe you can convince me that I do. And why use such an numbskull drug if you want to off yourself? Phenobarbital? Give me a break. If I wanted to do it, I'd ask for a morphine drip, go out on a wave of euphoria, take a pleasant journey down the river Styx."

"Because she used to threaten me with phenobarbital," said Archie. "She said she'd put it in my oatmeal if I made mistakes. I guess I think of it as poetic justice, using her ancient threat."

"I doubt she really wanted you dead. Sadists like to toy with their victims, not kill them outright," Bette said. "Who would she torment without you? She needed you, Archie; you were her pet project."

Ruby shifted in her chair. Gerard's clock ticked beside her. It said 3:09.

"That's true enough," said Archie. "She was eternally angry with my father for having the courage to hang himself."

"Well," Bette said, "you're right to think of drugs as the easy way out. Bullets or knives, now . . . that would be the John Wayne approach. Did you ever think of those?"

"I'm not taking the easy way out. I've tried and tried to find myself again, but you know as well as I do that there's no hope. Why not just admit it, and stop with the manly man baiting. I'd like to end my life more successfully than I lived it, and I'll end it without blood."

Ruby wanted to know how he'd managed to visit Bette's

office as Archie the adult, and for a second she nearly shouted the question into the phone. For a time, he'd been that way across the street, too. What was the trick to that?

"There's not *no* hope. I've seen lots of people fail, but also a few succeed," said Bette. "And you've got a child coming into the world. . . . How about thinking of someone besides yourself?"

She paused for such a long time that Ruby feared the connection might be lost. But finally Bette added, "Or maybe you don't think of the child as yours. Maybe you want nothing to do with him."

"I think of myself as the son of my father, of my father as his father's son. . . . So how can I not tremble with fear for my own star-crossed progeny? If there are curses on families, mine has one."

Ruby's body shook. That sounded far too much like Bob.

"Okay then, phenobarbital it is. . . . Let me see, where did I put my prescription pad?" Bette said. "Do you want to take it orally, or would you like me to inject it into one of those puffed-up veins of yours? It's a bitter pill to swallow, I hope you know, even if you smash it up and mix it with yogurt, as some people do. You don't want the last words you speak to be 'Phenobarbital, yuck!'"

"There's no need for sarcasm. Healing thyself of sarcasm might be a good goal for you, Mrs. Physician, before time infects you with the bitterness that is so often sarcasm's end."

That was both too irritating and too clever for Archie, and this time Bette heard it, too. "You can't be yourself for ten straight minutes, can you?" she said. "You can control the others but not him. I do have a problem with sarcasm, though; I freely admit it. It's been my cross to bear since I was young."

"When *I* was young, I was myself all the time. You were right to think that starting me over again at the age of that electric train might clear the path for a new beginning. . . . I thought it might, too, but it did not."

"That was Ruby's idea. She has a greater stake in saving you than the rest of us."

Ruby had been pressing her phone against her head with such great force that her ear began to throb. She tried to think how she could transfer the call to her cell, then listen to it while she raced across town, sprinting up the stairs and into Bette's office.

She looked at Gerard's closed door and then at his clock: 3:21. Where in God's name was Mr. Utterson?

When Archie made no comment about Ruby's stake in his survival, Bette asked him if he remembered the scene across the street with the book and the little girl. She asked him if he knew it had happened yesterday, knew whom he'd portrayed when he was there, and then seemed to change the subject before he could answer by asking him who, among all his various personalities, bothered him most.

"Too many questions and asked too quickly," Ruby said to herself, and Archie may have thought so, too, for he was quiet for a very long time.

But then he answered like a fellow clinician. "Let me take your last question first," he said. "You might think that Hyde bothers me most, but Hyde's no more trouble than your typical monster. He brays and badgers me whenever he can, but if you give a man like him enough rope, he'll imitate my father and hang himself."

Yes, thought Ruby, and Hyde hadn't been at Adriana's party.

"Long John Silver, then?" asked Bette. "I heard he was

bullying his way around, taking center stage with those birthday girls."

"Silver's worse than Hyde, it's true, for he charms his way into the hearts of those he later hurts," Archie said. "But Silver doesn't bother me most. Who bothers me most is the one who bothers me now, the one who says he came to give me hope."

"Dr. Okada!" Gerard called from his room, his voice as big as all outdoors.

"Are you recording this?" asked Archie. "What I want from you is phenobarbital. I don't want to be your case study, so if you're recording this, please turn off your machine."

Ruby got up and went to Gerard's door and opened it. "Practice your whispering now, Gerard," she said. "Doctor's orders."

Gerard's smile faded from his wide-awake face.

"Okay, I'll prescribe your pheno for you if you answer all my questions first," Bette said. "And I'm not recording anything. Only those engaged in it right this second will ever be privy to this conversation. What's more, I promise I won't speak about it to anyone else while you're still living on the earth."

"Which won't be long if I get that prescription. But I will answer your questions if you're quick about it. When a man decides to end his life, he doesn't mind saying why, but he also doesn't want to do it in a leisurely way. My father probably knew that when he hanged himself."

"You just now said that the one who bothers you most is the one who says he came to give you hope. Why do you think he's more toxic than the others? Is it because you think he gave you *false* hope?"

"No, no, no . . . Someone once told me that hope is just

hope, that none of it is false," said Archie. "That makes sense, does it not?"

"Yes, it makes sense, but if so, then what's so disturbing about him? Is it his fancy way of speaking, his lifetime of success that doesn't reflect your own?"

When Ruby whispered, "Such leading questions," Gerard's face perked back up.

"It is neither of those things," said Archie. "How can I begrudge him his success when I have taken refuge in the books he wrote? And how can I resent his way of speaking when he says what he means with such flair? Your questions show your lack of understanding."

"Ah," said Bette, "I think I'm beginning to understand. . . . He's flickering in and out of you right this minute. He bothers you most because you can't control him. I have to admit: He would bother me most, too, if he kept usurping my thoughts. With the others . . . well, I won't say you were malingering; that's too easy. . . . But you brought them out and used them when you needed them, right? They were like your own fucking private Mark Twains."

"Sometimes I think I'm getting stronger, that I can will him back out of me after only a sentence or two, that he can no longer stay for weeks at a time, like he did when he ruined Ruby's life," Archie said. "And if that were the case, I might try to go on, for with the others, yes, it's easier than I've admitted to keep them at bay. But what bothers me most isn't that he usurps my thoughts, and along with my thoughts my tongue. . . . What bothers me most is that he has decided that he wants to live fully again. He isn't here only to finish his stupid book, as he used to assure me was the case, but to keep on keeping on to the ripe old age of eighty-eight, doubling the years he had the first time. He didn't come to offer me *any* kind of hope, but to take my hope away. John Silver may come or Hyde may come, or Jekyll with his foolish ego, or Young Jim Hawkins with his youthful views of life. Some who come may pontificate, like Dr. Livesey, or come only once, like old Ben Gunn. . . . But with his desire to take forty-four years from me and add to those he's already had . . . Who can live with that?"

No one can, thought Ruby.

"I may be thick, but I still don't get it," said Bette. "You told me just a second ago that it's easier than you've admitted to keep the others under your control, but didn't you come to me in the first place, even go so far as to check yourself into our hospital, in order to be rid of them?"

"Let me put it this way," said Archie. "I have come to understand since I committed myself that the others come from the words *and worlds* I memorized when I was young, that they are inside of me, exactly like your own most vivid memories are inside of you. So though they may sometimes pop up unbidden like memories do, I can usually chase them away again by trying hard to think of something else. And also, if I want to, I can recall them. But *he,* the devil who wrote those words and invented those worlds, now wants to rewrite me and take my world as his own! And all I can think to do to stop him is to join my father and grandfather. And I want to do it *before* my baby is born, like my father's father did with him, and my father should have done with me. I don't want *my* four-year old son to find me hanging from a tree in our yard."

"So you were the one who found your father," said Bette. "That does not surprise me. But phenobarbital . . . Let me take a day or two to get things straight with the state of New

York; then I'll set you up with nice a morphine drip. How would that be?"

Oh, that Bette was crafty.

Come on, man, thought Ruby, give the lady the couple of days she needs!

Chapter Twenty

39

"I's THE SAME THING no matter which one of them said it," Gerard said. "Because Hal is in Mark and Mark is in Hal!"

"Don't get excited," said Mr. Utterson. "Okay, Mark might be in Hal, but Hal is not in Mark. Listen, Gerard, Mark Twain had no idea that one day Hal Holbrook would come along and dress like him and say the things he said. It's like Ruby's father when he made that painting hanging above you there, in homage to de Kooning. He knows he made it and you and I know he made it, but de Kooning himself didn't have a clue, because he was dead before Ruby's father even started it. . . . It's the same deal with Mark and Hal."

"No, it isn't! Dr. Okada's father didn't *become* the Koonering, he only copied him, but anyone can tell that Hal turns right into Mark. . . . We should all go see him. You can't believe how Mark Twain just comes strolling onto the stage! The Koonering doesn't do that. He just hangs there, staring at us."

Gerard's recovery seemed nearly full. They'd allowed him to come upstairs early on the evening of his second day home.

"Let me put it another way," Mr. Utterson said. "Do you

know that mask that Ruby and her father stuck out on the trunk of that tree house tree?"

"Yes," said Gerard. "They put it there when I was sick. What does she look like she's doing, Dr. Okada? You told me a little while ago, but I forgot."

Bette was due soon, so, anxious as she was, Ruby sat there listening to them. "She looks like she lives in the tree and came to the door when somebody knocked," she said.

"But she doesn't live in the tree; she only looks like it," said Mr. Utterson. "Just like Mark Twain doesn't live inside of Hal Holbrook."

"How do you know she doesn't live in there? What lives inside of trees could be anything at all. Sometimes foxes live in them, or skunks or badgers. . . . And wood is always living in them, 'cause that's where houses come from."

"That's where *lumber* comes from," Ruby's father said. "Someone has to build the houses."

When Ruby's front door opened and Bette walked in, all talking stopped. She had ridden over on her bicycle again, but this time she'd pulled it into the vestibule, taken some rags from the pockets of her rain slicker and laid them on the floor so it wouldn't get wet. The others hadn't even noticed that it had started raining again.

"No chance of your baby coming tonight?" Bette asked. "Not much movement from our little Mr. Stayput?"

"He stretches and turns and kicks," said Ruby. "Dr. Muir said that Monday will be D-day, inducementwise."

She wanted to sound normal, to stick with the subject at hand. In front of Gerard and Mr. Utterson, at least, she wanted to stay away from the conversation she had listened to on her phone.

"Hi, Bette, look at me!" Gerard said. "I'm upstairs again."

"You are indeed," said Bette. "You're a wonderful fighter, Gerard."

When she pulled her rain slicker over her head, her shirt came up, too, showing her midriff and the bottom of her bra. Mr. Utterson looked at the bra, while Ruby eyed the comfortable flatness of Bette's abdomen.

"Anything new to report?" asked Ruby's father.

He did not want to stay away from what Ruby had told him she had overheard, for what Bette had started calling Archie's "own private fucking Mark Twains," he now thought were reenactments, every step of the way. He was as convinced as Bette was that Archie could control them if he wanted to. Controlling Bob, however, seemed to be an entirely different matter.

"We've got him in a private room; he's eating a little. I've made a faux sort of record of his various pain levels and ordered some relief for it, starting tonight."

She gave Ruby a wry "in for a penny, in for a pound" sort of look.

"A room in your hospital?" Mr. Utterson asked. "Here we are again, then, back at the beginning."

Ruby hadn't yet told Mr. Utterson what she'd overheard. He had enough to deal with simply worrying about Gerard.

"Did you tell him we were going to see him?" Ruby asked. "That was our deal, remember?"

She hadn't seen Bette since Archie's readmittance, but she'd talked to her twice. The "we" who would go see Archie were Ruby and her father.

"Our deal was not that I would tell him; our deal was that you would go," Bette said. "Telling him anything now would only prompt another request for me to hurry up with the morphine. Look on the bright side, Rubes, there's no more talk of phenobarbital, which we couldn't control in the least."

"We're going over there now," said Ruby. "This can't wait until tomorrow."

She'd been sitting beside Gerard, beneath her father's version of *The Koonering*. She spoke, but she didn't get up.

"One thing is a little bit new," Bette said. "I learned from the duty nurse just a few minutes ago that someone came around to see him. Female, washed-out looking . . . The duty nurse told her what I said she could say—voluntary commitment, no visitors allowed for fourteen days. She left a cell phone number, believe it or not."

Bette was trying to speak cryptically, but cryptic wasn't her forte.

"I know who that was! It was Sister Mary Andrew!" Gerard said. "I can call her if you want me to, let her know my head is better. She was here on the day I fell down!"

"You can call her when the time is right, but that time isn't now," Ruby said.

She shook herself loose of her lethargy, and this time when she tried to stand, she did. Her view of the floor was obliterated by her abdomen's extension into the room.

"What time is it?" she asked. "Will you drive me over there, Gabriel?"

That was the best she could do in terms of including him, and when he said, "I will if I must, but why not let's do it tomorrow?" she asked her father to go outside and flag a taxi. Her father nodded and moved toward the door.

"Wait, wait," Mr. Utterson said, "I will certainly drive you if Bette will do me the honor of staying here with Gerard."

""I'd be happy to stay with Gerry," said Bette. "We can sit around and take it easy, make ourselves some sandwiches, watch a little TV."

"You'll be happy to stay with *Gerard*," Gerard said. "And *Gerard* get dibs over the remote control."

Chapter Twenty-one

40

"WEIGHT," RUBY TOLD THE DUTY NURSE when asked what the worst thing was about her pregnancy.

"Weight, and waiting. And moving around corners, when my belly goes first and my eyes come five seconds later. And the inability to take a deep breath. You know those cleansing breaths in yoga? I would kill for one of those right about now."

The duty nurse laughed, then sighed. "Count me out," she said. "I tell my boyfriend every week, that he'd better look elsewhere if he wants children."

The duty nurse, Ruby thought she remembered, was fifty-one years old. But she soon lost interest in Ruby, called Roger, the orderly that night, and went back to reading her magazine. At the elevators with Roger and her father, Ruby said, "Late night?" while they waited for one of the cars. Nine months and nearly two weeks earlier, Bob had said that to her. Late night. And now here she was.

"Not yet," said Roger, "but it will be by the time my shift gets done."

"Have you decided what you'll to say to him?" asked Ruby's father. "And do you know what you want from me?"

Mr. Utterson had driven them but was cruising around

outside, looking for a place to park. "I don't know what I want from anyone, Dad," said Ruby. "Let's just play it by ear, okay?"

The hospital's "voluntary commitment" wing was on floor five of the six-story building. Ruby's office had been on four, between Bette's and Dr. Spaulding's, and when they stopped there now, she had the urge to get off the elevator and go sit at her old desk in order to think things over for about the millionth time. She had no idea how she would react when she saw Archie, nor any strategy at all for defeating this idea of his to give up on life. Bette's ersatz morphine drip idea now seemed not only unethical but foolish. What could it do but buy them a little bit more time?

No one got on at floor four, so Roger stuck his head out and looked both ways. "Maybe someone's ghost pushed the button," he said.

On floor five, a couple of lights were out along the hallway—one in front of the elevator and another farther down. It gave the same impression of loss that Ruby remembered feeling when they'd visited Gerard to comb his hair that night, though at Roosevelt Hospital, the lights hadn't been burned out.

"It's the budget," said Roger. "If things don't start looking up, East Village Psychiatric will soon start laying people off, and I'll be number three."

The entire fifth-floor hallway seemed to sway back and forth under their feet, as if they were on the deck of the *Hispaniola*. As they followed Roger along it, Ruby took her father's arm. As with Archie's room at home, these rooms, too, had windows in their doors, though the glass was a half an inch thick, and crisscrossed with one-eighth-inch rebars.

But the windows were clean, at least, and music came from inside some of the rooms.

At the window of the first room, a young woman stood in very strict profile, the right side of her face so squarely aimed at them that there was no evidence that its left side existed at all. Her visible eye was wide and clear, her nose long and sharp, her chin pointed, and her lips primly pursed. She looked like the cross section of a healthy person, so perhaps her other profile was in polar-opposite relief. Ruby thought that she'd probably heard them coming and run to the window to pose that way. She glanced back several times as they made their way along the hallway, but the woman hadn't moved an inch.

The floor beneath them suddenly started chirping, as if built to warn the rest of those who'd committed themselves that visitors were coming, so that they, too, might leap into crazy positions. And, indeed, at each of the next four windows, people showed themselves off; a man with a hangdog expression, a finger in his mouth like a fishhook; an old woman licking her lips with a very long tongue, as if she were offering sex; a naked man with his hair standing up; and a middle-aged bottle blonde lip-synching "Knowing Me, Knowing You," the Abba song that played behind her.

Archie stood at the window of the last room but one on the right, his hair combed back in that pompadour again. But he retreated to the center of the room when Roger, without ceremony, unlocked and opened his door.

It should not have been without ceremony. Ceremony was all they had left.

"You've got thirty minutes, folks," said Roger. "I'll be right outside."

He closed the door and locked it again when they stepped into Archie's room.

""I told Bette I had to come here," said Ruby. "I don't know if she mentioned it or not, but that was our deal."

"I'm sorry for taking Bob away from you," said Archie. "I know you were in love with him."

"No question about it, but now it seems that Bob was you, so how am I to know whom I was in love with?"

Archie liked that response, and bowed in recognition of its generosity.

"He constantly pestered and threatened me, saying that I should be the one to leave," he told her. "He said that a love as rare as yours did not need me hanging around, that I would ruin it for you both."

"But in the end, that wasn't true," said Ruby's father. "For he wasn't free to love my daughter, just as her mother wasn't free to love me."

To Ruby's great astonishment and irritation, he pulled that Noh mask from the folds of his jacket as he spoke, holding it at arm's length, its white face facing Archie. Oh, why had he brought it here without telling her? To what end! Hadn't they had enough of that mask hanging around?

Irritated though she was, however, the mask's bright face made it instantly seem as if there were four of them in the room, a woman and her parents, come to confront the man who'd made her pregnant. The mask's blemish throbbed in the shadows of the room's poor light. She feared beyond reason that her father might try to make it speak, so she spoke first.

"What I still can't wrap my mind around is how I could have been so taken in," she said. "I'm sure there were signs;

there must have been signs. . . . But for those three weeks that he lived with me, I thought I'd found the man of my dreams."

"And yet he was the man of Archie's dreams, come unbidden, first to try to help him, then to take over his life."

Her father made the mask say this, confirming Ruby's fear.

"He didn't exactly come unbidden. He told me he came because he heard my cries," Archie said. "But all of that turned out to be lies. That is why I drove him out of your apartment, Ruby, and also, for a while, out of me. . . . The only thing he ever truly wanted was to finish his ridiculous novel, and he thought that I could be the one to help him do it, because I knew those other books of his so well. He worried all the time about Weir and Kirstie, but he didn't worry a second about you or me."

Ruby had the thought, despite herself, that her mother had probably heard her father's cries in long-ago Kyoto and willed his hand to render her face out of a block of cypress wood. *Hal is in Mark and Mark is in Hal!* . . .

"I have a question that I have been afraid to ask before," she said. "But now I am going to ask it. Why did you give me your house?"

She *had* asked the question of Mr. Utterson at Il Buco and hundreds of times thereafter, if only to herself. But she had never asked him. The question that nagged her far more, of course, was, Why had she taken it?

"It's easy to answer that," he said. "I gave you my house for selfish reasons, with the last of my 'self' that I could control. I wanted to watch my son grow up, and thought that I could do it more easily if I knew where my son was. Thus my feeble attempt to win you over by playing Cat Stevens. Thus that scene in your backyard, which had the ugly consequence of letting Bob back out."

"It wasn't such a feeble attempt," said her father. "Ruby always liked Cat Stevens."

There were only a few places to sit in Archie's room—the bed, the chair, the top of the desk. It was a lot like his room at home. Ruby went to sit on the desk in order to calm her growing worry that Yasuhiro might decide to fall out of her right then and there. She crossed her feet at the ankles and tried to press her knees together. "I'm glad to know you think of him as your son," she said. "My confession is that it hasn't occurred to me that you might think of him that way. I've never equated him to you and me, but always to me and Bob."

The front of her mother's mask looked away from her now. She saw only its hollow back and her father's grasping hand. *Oh, my grandson, don't be born yet,* she willed the mask to say.

"Because Bob was the man you loved, it was natural that you never thought of me," said Archie. "His eloquence, his manner, his fame . . . But I didn't begrudge him any of those things, as I think you know I told Bette."

"Bette ordered your morphine, you know, but do you think the unreality of that will be more palatable to you than your current one? Do you really want to die while feeling stoned?"

"Of course he does," her father said. "Who wouldn't choose euphoria? It's like choosing heaven over hell."

Ruby put her hand up, blocking her view of both her father and the mask. "Listen to me, Archie. I'm sorry I said what I said just now," she said. "I *did* think of him as your son once, but then I made the terrible error of forgetting it again. Do you remember what I said to you in our backyard?"

"You said, 'Your child is here, too. Would you like to come

touch him?' You said, 'Come put your hands on him. I bet he'll know your touch.' Those words gave me hope, but along with the hope came Bob, limping into my childhood room, and even ordering up a bath."

Ruby felt Yasuhiro kick and push. "If you'll allow me to say the words again right now, I promise upon my mother's grave that I will never forget them," she said.

She put her hand down and looked at the empty back of her mother's head, two of her father's fingers inside of it. She willed herself to breathe like she breathed in her breathing exercises. Archie, however, was still trying to answer her question.

"You also said, 'Can't you simply stay with me, Bob?' So you were talking to him, not me."

Her father suddenly put the mask down, as if he, too, had had enough of it.

"Come on, man. How did she know who she was talking to?" he said. "Can't she be forgiven for being confused, what with all the reenacting going on? If you're about to kill yourself, will you please admit first that this was all a period piece, an installation, a bit of crazy street theater going on?"

Oh, how indebted she was to her father! "Yeah," said Ruby, "come on, Archie, how about cutting me a little slack. After all, a moment after I said those things to you, who should come along but Dr. Livesey. What was a girl to do?"

"Livesey and the others were my weapons, my defense against a more intelligent man," Archie admitted. "I would not have lasted half as long as I did had I not had an army to call on."

"But you could call on them at will?" asked Ruby's father.

"Like I can pick up a brush, paint a picture, and have that picture hanging around?"

"Sometimes I could, yes, but sometimes they would just sort of be there, popping out unbidden when I was sitting around."

"And sometimes I can be halfway through a painting before I hardly know I've started it," said Ruby's father. "But it's interesting to think that the soldiers in your army all originally came from the mind of the man you called on them to help you defeat. It gets a little hard to follow if you think about it for too long."

When he smiled at Archie, Archie smiled back. "He created the soldiers in my army; I'll give him that," he said. "But for several generations now, if a Stevenson created anything at all, a Billingsly soon knew it better than he did."

"Your father and grandfather knew the books, too, then?" asked Ruby. "Did your Nana treat them like she treated you?"

"She invented her torture with my grandfather, honed it with my father, and perfected it with me. But she knew the books as well as any of us, so someone must have tortured her, too."

"Torture through works of art . . ." said Ruby's father. "I prefer to think of it as reenactments. But in any case, you outlived her, and I'm sure you can outlive her legacy, too, if you'll only give yourself that chance."

He put the Noh mask inside his jacket again, as if demonstrating how that could be done.

"If you try, I will help you constantly," said Ruby. "If you turn down the morphine drip, I will never speak to Bob again, even if he comes. That is my promise! And as for the characters from his books, it seems clear to me now all we have to do is send them back to the confines of their stories . . . whether slowly or quickly, only time will tell, but will you give yourself that chance? Will you give *me* that chance to help you?"

Roger, however, opened the door just then to tell them that Ruby had an urgent message. And that, in any case, their time was up.

Chapter Twenty-two

41

THAT MR. UTTERSON HADN'T COME inside the hospital, Ruby chalked up to parking problems, and gave it no more thought. The moment Roger ushered them out of Archie's room, however, he also handed her a note in Mr. Utterson's shaky script, saying that Gerard had suffered a relapse and that he had gone back home.

"He didn't want to bother you," said Roger. "He wanted you to have your time with that man."

Ruby found her phone, dialed Mr. Utterson's number, got no answer, and then dialed Bette's. "What kind of relapse?" she asked when Bette picked up.

"A bad one. I was helping him into his Mark Twain suit when he got a look on his face like he'd forgotten something, then froze from head to toe. He'd have fallen and cracked his head open again if I hadn't managed to lower him onto your father's ugly couch."

An image of Gerard's right hand came into Ruby's mind, forming the letter *C* again. She felt she could save him if only she could push a tumbler into it.

"Listen, Bette," she said. "If you take him to the emergency room, it'll be hours before someone sees him. Can you bring him over here? You're still number two, aren't you? Can't you call the duty nurse, get him in under 'indigent' or something?"

"I can try," said Bette. "You and your father stay put, then. I'll also tell Utterson what's going on. He just ran in."

When she hung up, Ruby told Roger only that Bette was bringing a new patient, and that she wanted him in the room next to Archie's. "I can't say why, but they need to be together tonight," she said. "Can you do that for us, Roger?"

It wasn't that she couldn't say why; it was that she didn't know why. But it seemed to her as vital as taking her next breath.

"Does this mean you are coming back to work here?" Roger asked. "Man, I hope so. We could use a little sanity around this place."

By the time the elevator opened twenty minutes later, spilling Bette and Mr. Utterson onto the fifth-floor hallway, Gerard between them on a gurney, Roger had made up the last room on the right. He had also pushed its window a few inches open to let in some of the cold fresh air.

"His breathing's slowed down," Mr. Utterson said, his own breathing coming in anguished spurts.

"There's oxygen and a defib machine right behind us," said Bette. "Dr. Singh is bringing them. I ran into him downstairs."

"He's not dead, is he?" asked Roger.

"No, he isn't dead!" Mr. Utterson yelled. "Good Christ, what a thing to say! Gerard! Open your eyes! Tell this man that Hal's inside of Mark as much as Mark's inside of Hal!"

For an instant, Ruby thought that Gerard might actually do it, for she remembered him surprising her yesterday, his voice as big as all outdoors. But he had no voice at all right now.

When she and her father ran to help, her father placed

her mother's mask on the gurney, not, she hoped, to give it meaning this time, but simply to get it out of the way. Still, now two faces stared at the boards that formed the ceiling along the hallway.

Once inside his room, Bette, Mr. Utterson, Ruby's father, and Roger all grabbed the sheet that surrounded the gurney, counted to three, then lifted Gerard over onto the bed. He was big and heavy and wide and short and squat—an alien come from a far better place than where Bob had come from.

"He's not dead yet, but he might be if Singh doesn't get here soon," Bette said. "Get on your phone and call him, Roger. His breathing's really shallow now, maybe even stopped."

"No need for that," Dr. Singh said from the doorway.

He pushed the defibrillator into the room, sent Roger back into the hallway for the oxygen tank, hooked up the defib pads, and yelled, "Clear!" like on television, making them all leap back.

When the machine uttered a *Zitttt!* Gerard's chest jumped.

"Blimey, Bette, why didn't you take him to Bellevue, or somewhere where they've got a proper crew?" asked Dr. Singh, but then he yelled "Clear!" again.

When the machine let out a second *Zitttt!* Gerard's eyes opened and shut.

"Come on, baby!" Dr. Singh said. "CLEAR!" he yelled again.

The machine was trying as hard as it could. Twice more when he said "Clear!" it responded faithfully, but Gerard's body jumped less each time. When Dr. Singh finally nodded and took off his gloves, Mr. Utterson said, "*What?* You can't stop now!" but Gerard's face and Ruby's mother's face, too, had begun to look equally inanimate.

Ruby reached out to touch them, the first one cold, the second one cooling fast. In the moments that followed, she tried to think *why* she had insisted that they bring him here, and not to someplace like Bellevue, while Mr. Utterson leaned against the room's far wall with Bette, who was trying to take him in her arms. Oh how Ruby despised herself! Where was her ability to feel and hurt and cry and love? Why could she do nothing but stand there, catatonic now herself?

No one else had cried yet, either, however. That was put on hold by Roger when he said, "It's happening again, Dr. Singh! The same old defib voltage screwup has opened all the doors along the hallway. Christ on a crutch, here come the walking dead."

Dr. Singh looked at him sharply, and then at Bette. "I told Spaulding thrice about the voltage issue, but he never did a thing about it," he said.

Gerard seemed more deeply offended by the fact that the power and sadness of his death had been taken from him by the hospital's faulty circuitry than by everyone's emergency medical failures. Ruby felt the offense of it, too, and looked at Mr. Utterson, who lifted his head off the wall, trudged back over to Gerard's bed, and put his hands on Ruby's where they now rested on Gerard's pale chest.

But no matter the level of anyone's offense, here came the walking dead, edging their way past Dr. Singh and into the room, in order to form a semicircle at the foot of Gerard's bed.

They were not the walking dead, of course, but people whom life as it is generally lived had abandoned. The man who hung his finger in his mouth was there, standing beside the profile girl, but his fishhook wasn't present, and she simply faced Gerard head-on. The woman who had licked her lips during all of the days of her commitment wasn't licking them, the naked man's hair had fallen down, and the Abba-loving woman had stopped her lip-synching, though they could dimly hear "Knowing You, Knowing Me," coming from down the hall.

The sixth member of the semicircle was Archie B. Billingsly, of course, who looked like he always looked when he wasn't invaded by somebody else.

Mr. Utterson and Ruby stood inside the semicircle, Bette and Ruby's father just outside of it, with Roger and Dr. Singh over by the door.

Gerard lay at the center of everything, with his hair still combed and his earring gleaming in the room's poor light. A breeze from the slightly open window pushed lightly against the sheet that covered the lower half of his body, and also moved his chest hairs back and forth.

Speech did not seem necessary, nor did anything need to be done in a hurry anymore. Death slowed the clock till its tickling meant nothing, just like in that clock store window. He *was taller by half than the old man himself* ran through Ruby's mind. Gerard wasn't taller by half than anyone, though in life he had weighed more than most.

Speech did not seem necessary, but when Archie spoke, everyone knew that this was what they had been waiting for. They shifted from foot to foot, some of them turning to face him, some of them coughing into their fists, like in church before the sermon.

What did Archie say? Quite simply, "Hey, Gerard, this thing about someone being inside of someone else . . . I've been giving that a lot of thought."

As he spoke, he grasped the padding between the thumb

and index finger of Gerard's *C* forming hand, pinching down hard. It was such a aggressive gesture, such a nearly violent one, that it lent a cruel vitality to his words.

Ruby kept her eyes on the clubbing of Gerard's fingers while Archie repeated his message. "This thing about someone being inside of someone else . . . This thing about someone being inside of someone else . . ." Each time he said it, he dug his fingers more deeply into Gerard's flesh, until the action began to encourage a bilateral cadaveric spasm along the line of muscle from the tips of Gerard's fingers to his biceps. His arms actually came a few inches up off the bed, as if some dead conductor were about to call his orchestra to attention.

And when that began to happen, Archie started saying something else.

"But listen, I don't want to think about who's inside of whom anymore," he said. "That's why I checked myself back in here, don't you know, so that I could put an end to the duplicity in my life. I've even got some morphine coming, to help me along with that. But you don't need to put an end to anything, Gerard, for you're one hundred percent yourself both inside and out. You're the only one like that that I have ever met in my life."

Without lessening his assault on the meaty part of Gerard's hand, Archie started drumming his free fingers along the flat expanse of Gerard's forehead. Really quite hard—rat-a-tat-tat!—like someone's frantic wartime Morse code.

"Hey, did you see *that!*" Mr. Utterson said, for there was no question that Gerard frowned, this time not in cadaveric spasm, but in obvious connection to the message he was getting. For a moment, Ruby thought he might say "Ouch!" but the next thing anyone heard was the voice of Dr. Singh, who was yelling, "Roger! Epinephrine!" plus that of the lip-synching woman, who threw her arms around the neck of the fishhook man and burst into tears.

Gerard's look was no longer inanimate, but one of mild surprise.

"I was dead, Mr. Utterson," he said. "Dead like nobody's business, and floating in a real warm bath."

"No, you weren't," said Mr. Utterson, "You were gone to Catatonia again, that's all, Gerard. But you were much more deeply into it than anytime before!"

"Nope, I was deader than a doornail. . . . Just ask Archie there; he's the one who brought me back."

When he lifted a stubby finger and pointed, Ruby turned in time to see the bottom of Archie's shirttail as he went out the door.

PART

FIVE

Chapter Twenty-three

$$\frac{42}{}$$

THIS IS THE STORY'S SHORTEST PART.

Mary Andrew Michaelsonsen appeared at Ruby's house at ten o'clock on the evening of November 13, carrying flowers and an oversized card. She would have left them on the stoop had Ruby's father not been pacing just within, heard her, and opened the door. She was in clean jeans, a clean blue work shirt, and a brand-new pair of Keds. He wore a work shirt, too, stained with blue paint. He also held a paintbrush in his hand, more blue paint on its tip.

"I heard the news," she said. "I feel the need to apologize, but I guess I thought I might avoid doing it in person by coming this late at night."

She flashed him the back of her wrist, where a watch would have been had she worn one. When he flashed his empty wrist back at her, his paintbrush made a small blue smile in the air.

"My daughter's asleep, but my grandson is awake. Would you like to meet him?" he asked.

He didn't clearly know who she was, for both of her visits to Ruby's office had occurred before his arrival. But he remembered her standing on the sidewalk after Gerard's fall, and sympathized with what she had said. It was his belief, too, that the Lord should raise all of them up: the weak, the lame, the meek, the good, the enablers and those they enable, the reenactors and those they bring back from the dead.

She peered at him through bright blue eyes—blue was the color of the hour—and, when he pulled the door more widely open, followed him into the parlor, where Yasuhiro Robert Okada Billingsly lay in a new bassinet on the top of the old piano.

The baby's eyes were open, but when his grandfather recited his litany of names, they fell back shut.

"We were sure that his birth would be difficult, but Ruby had no labor pains, no actual labor at all," he said. "He just popped out. 'Yasu' is what we'll call him. When I take him fishing, we will always go early. I will tell him he was born in his father's house at dawn."

She gave him her flowers and card, which he sat upon the coffee table—the flowers on their own, the card leaning up against his dripping teapot. When she reached into the bassinet to stroke the baby's cheek and push what little hair he had behind his ears, he decided he would stop her if she tried to pick him up.

"What if all this time we were all simply waiting for his birth?" she said. "That would be a relief, don't you think? A relief and a delight? Anyway, I should get going; there's a new delivery of Swiss steaks coming tomorrow morning. Will you please pass my apology along to your daughter and everyone else."

"What do you have to apologize for?" he asked.

He couldn't remember who had told him the story of her first two visits. It hadn't been Ruby and it hadn't been Bette, but he knew the story in all its various detail. Maybe it was just that, as he'd always suspected, everyone knew everything all the time.

"Is Gerard still in the hospital? I ask because I have a card for him, too," she said. "But I will take him food instead of flowers. Tomorrow I will take him a Swiss steak."

"He's there, but there's a 'Do Not Enter' sign on his door," said Ruby's father.

Mary Andrew Michaelsonsen laughed and laughed.

"But that only means 'Come in!'" she said. "It's the modern version of SOS, the universal cry for help."

43

BORN WITHOUT LABOR PAINS? Just popped out?

I beg your pardon! Ruby thought, for though the very instant of Yasuhiro's birth might have been smooth and calm, she had labored with him mightily for coming close to ten long months. Labored with him and argued with him, cajoled and pleaded with him . . . Did her father not know that?

As she sat at the top of the stairs listening to him talk to Mary Andrew, it was all she could do not to shout down her complaints, or hobble down to save her baby from the mystifying woman's touch. But she'd stayed both impulses, simply sat there listening, and gained a little satisfaction when her father mentioned Gerard's DO NOT ENTER sign, which she had penned herself just before heading home with Archie at something like 4:00 A.M.

Yes, with Archie, who slept in his childhood room again, that padlock gone from his door. Circles within circles, whirlpools within whirlpools, stories within stories . . . And yes— why not?—Mark inside of Hal and Hal inside of Mark.

After Mary Andrew left and her father stretched out on a pallet he had made for himself under the piano, Ruby crept downstairs to gaze at her sleeping son. The outside storms, Hurricane Sandy and its aftermath, had moved off to wherever storm graveyards are, and the inside storms had calmed enough for her to think that they might die soon, too, or confine themselves to her father's crooked teapot . . . tempests with no real meaning beyond the tender walls that housed them.

Was it an anticlimax for Yasuhiro's birth, after all these weeks of waiting, to have happened offstage, for him to have escaped the room that housed him by simply slipping through an open window and dropping to the ground? Should there have been screams and fireworks, bellowing and blood? Should his birth have equaled Gerard's rebirth, his miraculous return to life?

Dr. Muir had told Ruby that she would induce labor on the following Monday, or take him from her by Cesarean section, if necessary, due to his enormous weight. And Ruby had resigned herself to it. When they'd made a game out of guessing Yasuhiro's weight a day earlier, in fact, Mr. Utterson had come in highest, at twenty-two pounds. But Yasuhiro weighed only eight pounds, thirteen ounces, so perhaps while he'd been waiting to be born, he'd been dieting, knowing that he'd need to be svelte in order to affect his quick and easy birthing trick.

Ruby smiled at *svelte,* for as she looked at him now, he seemed pudgy. Her father, asleep on the floor, his head sticking out from under the piano . . . *he* was the one who looked svelte, with his sharp cheekbones and open mouth. He had been present for his grandson's birth, had, in fact, delivered him, if such a term is appropriate for a baby who essentially delivers himself. Ruby's father had been present, and so had

Yasuhiro's father, under the auspices of Archie the adult. What could be better than that? And in a way, Ruby's mother had been present, too, for when the baby slipped from between her far-apart legs, he came to rest on her mother's braided rug, her father's hands on either side of him.

There hadn't been time for a more sanitary birth, but when they took Yasuhiro to Dr. Muir's office later that morning so that she could check him and weigh him, he got a "clean bill of health." Those were the words that Dr. Muir had used, and afterward, when they got back home at noon, the baby asleep and everyone else exhausted, Archie said that he had finally decided that that was what he wanted, too—a clean bill of health. He reminded Ruby of her promise never to speak to Bob again, even if Bob should come around, and when Ruby made the promise yet again, Archie promised her, in turn, that he would do the same with Jekyll or Hyde or Long John Silver . . . with all of those who had bothered him for so long. He promised Ruby and he promised Ruby's father and he promised his newborn son.

Later, he confided only to Ruby's father that he thought he would be rid of them anyway, since the night before at the hospital he had done his best to drum them into Gerard.

Now, in the parlor, just as Ruby lifted Yasuhiro from his bassinet, she sensed a presence behind her and turned, to find Guido and Francesca standing side by side. She'd forgotten Guido's shot far too often lately and would take him to the vet soon, in order to have his ketones checked. She would take Francesca, too, since Francesca had never been there. A healthy dog and cat would be a start. . . .

"Hey," she said. "Do you two want to meet this guy? He's the newest member of our family, got here just a while ago.

His name is Yasuhiro, which means 'abundantly tranquil.' That would be nice for a change, don't you think, to have things calm and easy around the house?"

When Guido and Francesca looked at each other, Ruby sat down on the twisted green couch and waited for them to come to her. They were tentative creatures, this dog and this cat, but had formed a sort of pact, until now they were abundantly tranquil themselves.

"Come on," she said. "He won't bite. You are both going to love him as much as I do, I can tell."

Guido came first, his eyes as round as little cat marbles.

"Do you know what's funny? What's funny is that here we are, having gone through all we've gone through, yet nothing much has changed. Archie's will still have his battles to fight, I still don't have any money coming in, and Gerard . . . well, we hope that Gerard will be coming home soon. I guess we'll have to see how that works out."

The cat and the dog were next to her now, sniffing Yasuhiro's soft blue baby blanket. Guido put a furry paw up over the blanket's edge and touched the baby's forehead with it. His touch left a bit of a shadow, not to say a pall, which departed when the paw did, but there was no question that Ruby had seen it. When she stood again with her baby, Guido and Francesca backed up.

"We should all go do what my dad is doing. No one gets enough sleep around here," she said.

When she started out of the parlor, ready to take the baby upstairs, she bumped against the coffee table, knocking over Mary Andrew Michaelsonsen's card. She nearly ignored it, nearly didn't right it again, until Francesca picked it up in her mouth.

"No, Francesca, that's not nice," she said. "It's someone's good wishes, and we could certainly use them. *Everyone's* good wishes might not be enough."

When she held her hand out, Francesca dropped the card into it, then waited for a pet. Gerard had trained her well. Ruby tucked the card under her arm.

In the hallway, she noticed that the front door wasn't latched, that her father hadn't closed it properly when he let Mary Andrew out, so she pushed it shut with her hip, heard a solid click, then went into the living room to look out the window, on the chance that Mary Andrew might still be lurking about.

This time, she was not. Bank Street was windless and dark and rainless for once. She sat down on the spot where her braided rug had been—it was now rolled up, ready to go to the cleaner's—lay back, put her baby on her flattening abdomen, and took the card out from under her arm.

It was not exactly a good-wishes card, nor was it addressed to her. It was addressed, of all damned things, to "Robert Louis Stevenson." Perhaps she thought that this was Yasuhiro's name, though Ruby'd heard her father say it properly to her when she arrived. Yasuhiro. Robert. Okada. Billingsly. Two parts Ruby, one part Archie, and yes, okay, one part Bob, but only one part, not enough to constitute a quorum.

"Can you believe that woman?" she asked her sleeping baby, but she opened the card anyway. What else could she do, throw it away?

"November 13, 1850, to December 3, 1894, and now November 13, 2012 to . . . I wonder what your death date will be this time?" said the card. And then, written at its bottom were the words

"Happy, Happy Birthday Baby," just like in that Tune Weavers song.

Ruby reached over to pull down that inscribed edition of *Treasure Island* from the bookshelf, and sure enough Bob's dates inside of it were just as they were on the card. *November 13, 1850–December 3, 1894.*

"Really? November thirteenth? That's what you were waiting for?" she asked her baby.

But he was asleep on a soft bed of postpartum flesh, which rose and fell with every one of Ruby's breaths.

44

FORTY-FOUR SHORT SECTIONS, one for each year of Robert Louis Stevenson's life. But no more going forward. This was Ruby's firm decision.

Another decision, an utter determination, was that she *would not now, nor would she ever,* suspect her son of being Bob. Lots of people were born on November 13—Edward III of England, Oskar Werner, the actor who had played Jules in *Jules et Jim* . . . She had looked them up. And all three Archie Billingslys were born on different dates.

Still, she slept badly that night, with Yasuhiro cuddled beside her in her bed. To do such a thing was against what all the baby books said, but for this one night she didn't care. She needed to keep an eye out for shadows on his forehead, or for the comings and goings of thoughts put in his head by someone other than himself.

She would never accuse him of being anyone else, but how could she not be vigilant? It would be child abuse not to notice such things, would it not?

Meanwhile, over in his room on the fifth floor of East Village Psychiatric, behind that door with the DO NOT ENTER sign that Ruby had made for him, and in front of Mr. Utterson, who nodded in and out of sleep in a bedside chair, Gerard sat up with several pillows behind his back, his knees bent under the covers, staring down at a yellow legal pad that, at his request, Mr. Utterson had brought him.

He wrote down the following words as carefully as he could and using his best penmanship:

> *"Kirstie, indeed!" cried the girl, her eyes blazing in her white face. "My name is Miss Christina Elliott, I would not have ye to ken, and I daur ye to ca' me out of it. If I canna get love, I'll have respect, Mr. Weir. I'm come of decent people, and I'll have respect. What have I done that ye should lightly me? What have I done? What have I done? O, what have I done?"*

Gerard looked at what he'd written, then at Mr. Utterson.

"He told me I should get a running start, so I guess that's what these words are," he said, "but I don't know what most of them mean. I do understand that Kirstie wants to know why people aren't nice to her, 'cause that's what I always wanted to know, too, till you came along, Mr. Utterson. . . . You and Dr. Okada and Francesca and Guido and Dr. Okada's father . . . And Bette, too, I guess."

He looked back down at the words again. "'*I would not have ye to ken, and I daur ye to ca' me out of it*' doesn't make a bit of sense to me," he said.

Mr. Utterson took the paper that Gerard extended to him,

yawned, and read the words himself. "I don't know," he said. "I'm English, not Scottish, and I haven't been there for a very long time. . . ."

But then he sat up straight. "Hold on!" he said. "*Who* told you that you should get a running start? Was someone in here while I was taking my nap?"

≈≈◎≈≈

Meanwhile, back at the Bank Street house, Ruby and her baby were finally sleeping soundly in her bed, while Ruby's father slept under the piano down in the parlor. Archie had tried for a while to sleep, too, but gave up and came down from his room to stand in Ruby's doorway and look in at his son and the mother of his son, not to say the woman who loved him.

He leaned against the doorjamb, his hands in his pockets.

≈≈◎≈≈

Meanwhile, over in his fifth-floor room at East Village Psychiatric, Gerard was having trouble answering Mr. Utterson's question, though Mr. Utterson asked it two or three more times, progressively more demandingly. "*Who* told you that you should get a running start? Was someone in here while I was taking my nap?"

He should have known better than to insist—Gerard did not like tension in anyone's voice.

≈≈◎≈≈

Meanwhile, back in the Bank Street house, just as with Guido's and Francesca's arrival in the parlor some hours earlier, Ruby sensed a presence nearby and opened her eyes, to see Archie in her doorway. When he saw her see him, he took his hands from his pockets, spread them out, and opened them, palms toward her.

Ruby looked at Yasuhiro. "Here's comes Papa," she said.

Meanwhile, over in the fifth-floor room at East Village Psychiatric Mr. Utterson realized his folly and calmed back down again while Gerard wrote the following:

> *Archie ran to her. He took the poor child in his arms, and she nestled to his breast as to a mother's, and clasped him in hands that were strong like vises. He felt her whole body shaken by the throes of distress, and had pity upon her beyond speech. Pity, and at the same time a bewildering fear of this explosive engine in his arms, whose works he did not understand, and yet had been tampering with . . .*

This is the final *meanwhile*,

Meanwhile, over at the Bank Street house, when Archie accepted Ruby's invitation to come sit on the edge of the bed, Ruby, whose hands were like vises, too, used them to take him in her arms, tipping his head so that they looked into each other's eyes.

There then arose from before him the curtains of boyhood, and he saw for the first time the ambiguous face of woman as she is.

Acknowledgements

THANKS TO the University of Nevada, Las Vegas, and to Black Mountain Institute for funding research activities during the writing of this novel. Thanks to Joseph Appel for answering my questions about various psychiatric conditions, including dissociative identity disorder, and to the late John McCormack, of the US Marine Corps, for his letter to my grandparents upon the death of their son, Jack W. Morgan, in Guam, in July of 1944. I used part of Mr. McCormack's letter as if it were written by one of my characters. A big thanks to Joseph Langdon for retrieving this novel for me from the bowels of the Internet when I thought it lost forever. Unending gratitude to my wife, Virginia Wiley, for reading draft after draft of this work, and to my daughter and son, Pilar Wiley and Morgan Wiley, for support, comment, and critique. Blessings upon Erika Goldman and the staff of Bellevue Literary Press for believing in *Bob Stevenson,* in all his various guises.

Bellevue Literary Press
New York